Imagine Anywhere

FOREIGN FOREST

To my loved ones, this book is for you. Let it help you escape from reality for a bit. However, if fate and all else fail to bring you home, you need only ask yourself the questions: when, where, and why, followed by reciting the incantation written on the last page of this book.

Table of Contents

Prologue

Once upon a time, there was a carpenter named Samuel Wilson. Though he was highly ordinary in every sense of the word, his passion for carpentry was respected amongst the locals. They would often honk their horns and wave as they passed by his house, where they'd see him lost in thought, focusing on his next great creation. He felt alive when he was in the middle of a project, and the attention he received from people passing by convinced him to establish his furniture shop, *The Ark*. Many locals would frequently pop into Sam's shop looking for something that would strike their fancy. His furniture was a sight to behold; beautiful knick-knacks and carefully bent and stained woods were evenly spaced around the warehouse he rented for his shop. Luckily, it also came with wide windows in the front that allowed people to see his newest creations. Though some of Sam's pieces may have also looked vintage, they felt sturdy. He was diligent and would even take people's discarded furniture and restore it to its original condition for a fee; this was mainly how he supported his family. He lived in a big, modern home on the corner of Acacia Street, not far from downtown but a bit higher up elevation, tucked away with newer housing developments in the hills around it. There he had a wife and son waiting for him at the end of each day.

Years further into his successful career of helping others furnish their homes, Sam was ending his workday at the shop and getting ready to head home. After blasting the radio all day, crickets were a relief to hear. It was late. He let out a huge sigh, and gravel crunched under his worn-out work boots as he walked towards his truck. There, he was met by a suspicious older man leaning on the hood.

"I don't intend on taking much of your time, but I have a proposition that might benefit us both," said the stranger as he lifted his elbow from the hood, leaving a dent. It was hard to tell if this dent had already been there, though. Sam's truck was frequently used for work.

"How can I help you, sir?" asked Sam. Exhausted yet insistent on being kind, he listened to the older man's proposition, mainly because he wanted to fast forward to the end of the story so he could decline and continue his departure.

"I find myself in need of a table—a circular one. Made with this wood that I've collected from my family plot. It is to my understanding that you can work with delicate materials, yes? Your help would be excellent, then. After it's complete and I have it in my possession, I will make you a rich man. This I swear to you, on my life."

The carpenter looked puzzled. What type of riches could this elderly man loitering in the parking lot possibly have that he can offer? Though home was beckoning to him in his thoughts, he listened intently and eventually agreed to the stranger's proposal. With the idea of a better life for him and his family, Sam then followed his new patron an hour out of town to a cabin deep in the woods, where few seemed to have lived because it was pitch black out there. He picked up the wood as requested, said his goodbyes to the gentleman after getting his contact information, and returned to his workshop to drop it all off before heading home in the early hours.

It took about a month before Sam finished this project. Most of that time was spent in contemplation of what exactly the significance of this table will be, that it can bring him riches unlike any other table he had made. He was befuddled, but finished building and sanding before he decided it was shaped perfectly. One morning, he woke up excited as ever to add a final layer of varnish to the table. It was his favorite part of the process: sealing his magnum opus with an everlasting final touch. Sam was eager to see his patron's reaction, so he called, letting him know his table was ready for pickup. Within minutes, there was a shadow outside the shop's translucent door, and a figure entered, the door's bell jingling as he swung it open. His thin feet making little noise, much like a bird, whose hollow bones allow so.

"Well, I hope it's everything you wanted. I'll admit, the wood was very... difficult to work with. Though, I do hope it's to your liking, sir! Now about payment?" said Sam.

The mysterious man strolled around it, observing it from every angle with a stoic look on his tired, wrinkled face. He crouched and observed the underside, before resurrecting and wiping the table with his finger. He smiled. "This will do. My good sir, what you've done for me is priceless. Therefore, I feel no problem giving you everything you deserve."

The old man, who had reached his hand into his pocket and pulled out a bag, met eyes with the carpenter. He closed them, tossed a bag into the air, and laid a finger on the table. It was thought that the old man muttered something, as well, but Sam couldn't make it out. He was in shock. The old man vanished as if he had never been there, and he had taken the table with him! In his place, a bag now lay on the floor.

Sam picked it up and was astonished to find a handful of jewels inside that were undoubtedly worth a fortune. He couldn't help but wonder what the stranger wanted this table made for. In Sam's mind, the man could only be a magician.

* * *

After his sudden departure from the carpenter's shop, the old man was now back in the basement of his home. He sighed, relieved to have finally retrieved his table. It was a vital piece in something that had been the focus of his studies for quite some time. Unfortunately for him, his short-lived moment of peace was suddenly interrupted by a subtle knock on the door. The magician scoffed, got up, and opened it to see a familiar face.

His thirteen-year-old grandson, Shiloh, was staring up at him with a look of confusion. "Grandpa, why are people throwing cabbage at our house? I opened my window for a minute, and it's not exactly the greatest smell in the world."

The old magician and his family lived in a two-story home on Coffee Road, just two blocks east of downtown. His neighborhood wasn't the grandest, but it was quaint, ordinary, and suburban—not exactly a prime location for magic and wizardry.

Not wanting to interfere with his work, his wife and grandson would stay out of the basement most of the time. And if anyone ever got caught loitering outside the basement door, the old magician would become very displeased, often muttering mean things underneath his breath that you could still hear because of the crack under the door.

Though the old magician hadn't always preferred such isolation, he was now consumed by it, thanks to his obsession with the table. The smell his grandson had mentioned before was from the rotting cabbage outside his house thrown by those who weren't particularly fans of his magic shows. These days, people seemed to laugh at the failure of others, and normally it would drive the old man mad to be laughed at. However, he had already noticed the foul smell when he returned from the carpenter's workshop. For once, he felt intoxicated by it, knowing that all his troubles would soon be gone forever.

Fetching this table was life-changing for him. He would use it alongside a book he got in a pub, salvaged from a chess game he'd won against a stranger.

Upon gifting him the book, the stranger was reluctant to divulge any information about it. However, after seeing how nonchalant the magician was wielding the book and its pages, he felt inclined to tell him the truth. This stranger had told him that the tome was as old as time itself and made from dark magic that most could not bear to witness. This, of course, intrigued the magician an enormous deal. Simply holding this artifact in his hands, the magician could immediately feel the energy emanating from it. It was light, too. Too light. It took little effort to pick it up.

Excited to begin examining the book, the magician returned home to sleep until the following day, but it felt like his dream that night had lasted a whole year. Keeping the book so close to his bed must have twisted his dreams, seeing only the visions the tome allowed him to. These visions didn't convey much detail; rather, they were more like plain images devoid of context. Nevertheless, each passing shape or figure was linked to each other in ways he couldn't explain. He saw himself in a void, a pitch-black plane where only he existed, alone with his thoughts. The eeriness of perfect solitude began to eat at him, but not for long. Inside the darkness with him appeared an eye, whiter than he remembered white to be. It was blinding, but as he focused on it, he noticed it was looking right back at him. This realization was disturbing. Something was in here with him. These dreams he'd experience while sleeping next to the book revealed their primordial nature to him, showing him images in a sequence intended to convey its message simpler than words ever could. The message was understood at a certain point upon waking up from this dream, though this fleeting insight quickly vanished. The magician's sheets were covered in sweat. He sighed and looked at his nightstand, relieved to be awake yet unnerved to see the book still sitting there. Suddenly, it flipped open. There on the page, staring right back at him, was an eyeball. The magician gasped! Was this real? The eye shut and then vanished without a trace, and in its place appeared a set of runes, though they looked unlike any he had seen before. A shrill voice then came from the book, and it muttered a phrase the magician recognized as Latin: *Quod est superius est sicut quod inferius.* He copied what he saw on another sheet of paper that he had in his bedside drawer. He wondered how what he had just seen was possible. Going back to bed shortly after, he dozed off quickly, dreaming of what he might do next regarding the book and table.

The following day, the magician brought out a long obsidian blade that he had found when he was younger on a hiking expedition. He used his favorite pen, which used green ink, to draw the runes around the outside edge of the table, then proceeded to carve them out using the blade. He didn't know what was to come, but he knew what he wanted to happen. Whether it would work out or not, however, he was unsure. He was to craft an enchanted table that would bend time and space to the will of whoever sat at it. So, he did, and throughout his time with it, it became like an extension of him. But once he completed his carvings, the book, as old as time itself, spontaneously burned to dust in a matter of seconds.

"No!" the magician cried, though his spiraling thoughts were soon centered by a loud low-frequency hum coming from behind him. The hairs on the back of his neck stood up. He turned around to see the table, floating there weightlessly, slowly rotating in an eerie fashion. The runes he had just carved were now glowing with a bright, white light.

This intrigued the magician. He grabbed his bag of tools and a few books without breaking eye contact with the table, and then carefully went to touch its wooden surface out of curiosity. Next thing he knew, he had vanished along with the table, and the rest was much like a dream.

He went on adventures with this table using books. Yes, books. Touching the table while lying a book on its surface would send those connected to the it into another dimension parallel to their own. With a setting and plot based on the book—down to the most intricate details—it was hard for the magician not to get lost in these worlds, and many times he did. Though the table would always reappear to him at some point or another. The magician used his vast library to explore his minds wildest dreams, and with each book he entered, he could control the table's powers with less and less effort. Each book felt like a different dream. He could leave each "dream" by finding the table, touching it while closing his eyes, and saying the Latin phrase he had discovered from the book which was now just a pile of dust. After the first few books, he realized he didn't have to say the incantation as much as he had to think and believe it. It translated to "as above, so below."

After many months of exploring throughout his book collection, the magician whom we may now know as Everett Evans, the failed yet soon-to-be recognized magician and grandfather, had the passing thought of writing a book of his own. Though, the subject matter of which was something that, he assumed, would come to him at a later time. So, he discarded the idea for the time being.

One evening, after getting home from a doctor's appointment, Everett had a moment where he forgot where he was and how he had ended up there. These brief lapses of memory would continue as the weeks progressed. After his appointment, the doctors called and explained to Everett's wife that he had been diagnosed with mild Alzheimer's. This meant he may soon begin forgetting recent events, becoming frustrated more easily, and losing items more frequently, such as his keys, though he could retain a positive demeanor at times. The disease was stealing control of a part of him. This crushed his wife to know. Everett didn't know because she didn't want him to. She loved Everett and didn't want to lose him, though she knew that his life was not in her hands. She comforted him on most nights when he'd come back up from his work downstairs, and as the months went by, she noticed that his moments of unpredictable mood and behavior only became more frequent.

Everett was sitting in his basement study one night when he suddenly decided to get rid of his table. He was losing his mind, and he knew it, but when he entered a book using the table's magic, he felt alive, more so than he had been before he entered. It was as if the magic of the table rejuvenated his youthful spirit while inside the books, though he still appeared a shriveled, old man. Eventually, though, his travels throughout the books left him reminiscing about his wife. His adventures were amazing, but still, felt rather lonely. He understood that, if he was to regain any sense of normality in his life again, he had to pass his creation off into the hands of someone he trusted.

The following day on his walk around the neighborhood, he saw a sign that said, "Yard Sale." Perhaps he should have his own and also have the table out. Besides, a garage sale would allow him to give it to the right person if fate decided they should come. After a long day of many people asking about the table, among other things he had out for his garage sale, he had his eyes on a blonde woman with her sights set on the table.

She was walking around it, dragging her finger along the runes. She approached him a moment later and asked, "How much did you want for this table? It's lovely! It's got a spooky vibe, yeah? It'd be a perfect writing table for me. How much?"

At first, he choked on his response, but said, "You aren't C. J. Wingate, perhaps, are you?"

The woman blushed. "Yes, that's me. Are you a fan?"

"Indeed, I am," he replied. He hadn't realized it was her until this moment. He had read many of her books before while using the table and could explore them in unique ways. "Big fan of your work. You create beautiful worlds in your books."

Ms. Wingate smiled and replied, "Thank you so much. I'll sign anything if you have it."

"I'm sorry. How rude of me! The table. I would love for you to have it for free. This miraculous table was made from the wood of my family plot. You see, it was made just for me, but I have no use for it any longer, so I think you would be the best person to give this table to."

That was it. The table found itself jammed into the back of the writer's SUV, and Everett shed a tear as he watched it disappear into the sunset. She was able to have it unloaded and in her house by later that night.

Everett felt good knowing that the table would be in the best hands possible. After all, he was an avid reader of Ms. Wingate's novels and was delighted to see her pay any interest to his garage sale. Everett's journey with the table had now come to an end. He had deduced the science behind it all, he figured. The books would inadvertently create parallel dimensions stemming from the real world. Using the table and its magical powers would send whoever spoke the incantation into the new dimension that resembled the universe of the chosen book. It was all quite simple, Everett thought. Though one thing was still missing.

Days passed, but Everett's mind didn't stray far from the enchanted table. One day, he had an idea about the perfect story for his book that he wanted to write. It was about a time outside of time; a memory he had forged not by witnessing an event but by will of thought. He reflected on this "memory" often. Of course, this book was his favorite to explore. His wife and grandson didn't see much of him for this very reason.

After writing no more than just a few paragraphs, he called it complete and laid the tiny booklet out on his desk. With a sigh of relief, he reclined in his desk chair and fell right to sleep.

The following Friday, Ms. Wingate was left startled when she came home after grocery shopping to find her dining room in shambles. Her new table missing and her laptop on the floor, miraculously undamaged. This was strange, as she had remembered locking up before leaving the house. She was distraught for a whole three minutes before she realized that she needed to finish the book she's writing by a specific deadline. She chalked it up to a possible non-violent home invasion that she nearly escaped in time by leaving to the store, yet convinced herself she was safe and didn't call the police. She decided that she would wait and tell her husband when he got home later that evening. For now, she would have to make do with writing on her liftable coffee table in the living room, though she was curious where her new one might have gone.

* * *

Everett retired to his study for the next few days, not to be seen by anyone again. One night, his wife, Faith, woke up curious as to where her husband had gone. Worried, she went to check on him in the study, but opened the door only to find him missing. Faith continued to search the house high and low, but sadly found nothing that would give her a sign as to where Everett might be. He was gone. Eventually, she fell asleep on the couch in the living room, exhausted from her efforts. Her grandson woke up to get a glass of water and noticed her. It was puzzling, and he probably would've investigated it further had he not been half asleep. When the clock reached midnight, however, the table reappeared in the magicians study, but with no magician.

This was how the magic table came to be. The carpenter, the magician, and the writer all played a vital role in its creation and enlivenment. This table was indeed magic: forged by the labor of a carpenter, enchanted by a magician ahead of his time, and briefly owned by a writer who could "create worlds," so to speak, just by writing them down and using a little imagination.

There was no telling the destiny of the table, yet it would stick around for generations to come. Now, this isn't a tale about witches and wizards. It's more real than that. This is the much darker story of a twisted, tangled journey made by three young adventurers: the children of the carpenter, the writer, and the magician.

Chapter 1
Just Like a Worm

It was only October, but all the leaves had already fallen off the trees and filled the air with the sound of crunching underneath peoples' feet. The schoolyard had a warm tint to it, as if the sun in the distance set fire to the floor of dead leaves below it. Shiloh was getting a headache. He was exhausted from lack of sleep. His head rested against the car window in the backseat of his grandma's sedan as she took him to school that morning. They pulled into the school parking lot, and Shiloh got out of the car, but not without a smooch on the cheek by his sweet, old grandmother. He loved her very much, and there was no doubt she loved him. Shiloh waved goodbye and walked into the school to attend his first class of the day: English. He wasn't excited, though. He hated being in eighth grade.

The teacher, Mr. Moonward walked towards the front of the classroom to address the students as they took their seats.

"Alright, I'm giving you all five minutes. By then, everybody should done with their entries. The topic is on the board."

Each morning in English class, the students had to write down an entry in their journals regarding whatever topic was written on the class chalkboard. Today's journal topic was "What is your biggest fear and why?" This was something that made Shiloh nervous. He did have a lot of worries, though this appeared to be one of the only times that would actually give him an advantage over his peers. He finished his journal entry and left the classroom before anybody else, like a bat out of hell.

Already in his art class, Shiloh was unpacked had his paper and pencil out before the bell rang. After all, art had always been his favorite subject.

The classroom had tables with assigned seats that each sat two students. Shiloh sat next to Emma Wingate, on whom he had a massive crush, though he didn't think she knew. The teacher assigned the class the task of painting a picture from memory. After that they'd each been given a white canvas, and then everyone began working on their projects. It was only thirty seconds until the class clown, Robert, had painted a penis. This sent the classroom into hysterical laughter. The teacher tossed his canvas away and sent him to the dean, but not without an applause from the students. Once the rest of the children had finished, the students swapped their artwork with the classmate next to them. The teacher instructed them to explain their memory along with its relevance to the painting. Little did Robert know that he was saved the embarrassment of that explanation. As the other students chatted over their paintings, Emma and Shiloh were hesitant. Emma decided to break the silence.

"This was my mom and I at her first book signing," she said. "That's me on her shoulders there, see?"

Emma stared at the painting as if looking into an old photo reminding her of a moment she deeply missed. Shiloh could feel her longing to relive that memory but was trembling with nerves at the fact she was talking to him. Usually, they didn't say more than a few words to each other, so the day's exercise had certainly changed that.

"That's pretty," Shiloh replied. "My grandpa loves your mom's books."

Emma blushed. "What's up with yours?"

Shiloh chuckled and then looked at his painting. "It's just my parents at the beach, well… and me. I'm no Van Gogh or anything. I miss them, that's for sure."

Shiloh's parents had passed away, and though everybody at school had heard from someone or another, no one ever dared to mention it around him.

* * *

It had always been his parents' dream to see the sights and go on a train ride along the coast to celebrate their anniversary. So, one day, they finally booked the trip. The morning of their departure, Shiloh stood by the front door, watching them pack.

"Please stay," Shiloh whimpered.

His dad picked him up and put him on his shoulders. "It's only for the weekend, buddy."

He handed Shiloh over to his mother, who kissed him on the forehead.

"Don't eat too much cereal or bug your grandparents too much," she said. "They're in charge. You know that don't you?"

She messed up his hair and chuckled as they stepped out the door and headed to the train station.

* * *

That evening, Shiloh's grandmother was knitting and watching the evening news.

"This just in: A high-speed train collision has happened today, killing hundreds and injuring thousands."

She was horrified to see that it was the same train Shiloh's parents had booked for their anniversary trip. Apparently, a driver fell asleep at the wheel while caught in traffic crossing the railroad tracks. It seemed they did not wake up in time to escape the path of the oncoming train. Upon hearing this, Faith was left speechless and in tears. She had no idea how she'd break the news to Shiloh. So, she didn't. Or at least not until after a month had passed of Shiloh asking why his parents' weekend trip had turned into a month-long one. She could barely hold back her tears just telling him the news. What's sad is that the boy didn't even cry. He simply walked to his room, put his headphones on, and started drawing. Shiloh's reaction was worrying to his grandmother. She always kept an eye on him after that.

* * *

The boy had never been the same after hearing the truth, though. Sadly, he had even forgotten what his parents had looked like. He lived with his grandparents permanently now, and as the years passed, any memories of his real parents became blurry, which made him number to it all. He stopped talking to his schoolmates as often, and instead kept to his books in the library, or art class, whenever the teacher would let him in.

Back in class, as Shiloh was explaining the subject matter of his painting, Emma noticed the pain in his eyes.

"I'm sure they'd be proud of you, Shiloh."

He looked over at her and noticed the warmness of her eyes and the luster of her lips.

"Th-Th-Thanks Emma," Shiloh said, choked up.

The bell rang, and, as usual, he ran out of the classroom before anyone else. Her eyes followed, full of wonder as he bolted off. It was time for recess, and there was a spot in the yard where Shiloh preferred to sit and read—a patch of shade under a willow tree on the edge of the grounds. Yet he would much rather stay indoors to avoid people—especially Logan Wilson.

Logan was a bully. He would always bother Shiloh whenever he'd get the chance. When they got out for recess, he saw Shiloh reading a book under the tree and decided to go over and bug him.

"What's up, Shy Guy? How's it feel not having any friends?"

"Says the dude that walked over here by himself," replied Shiloh, more pointedly than usual.

Logan didn't like being outwitted. For him, it was a one-way street. He was usually the snarky one, yet Shiloh was quicker to respond, always on alert when Logan came around. That's because Logan didn't seem to care much for the feelings of others. Well, except for their classmate, Emma. Since the first grade, he had found her attractive, yet never found the courage to tell her. Instead, he would let out all his pent-up energy on the weaker kids around the school, Shiloh becoming his primary target.

"Get off of me!" Shiloh exclaimed from under Logan, who now had Shiloh pinned to the ground.

Shiloh was throwing punches left and right into the air that didn't seem to connect to anything.

"You wish, loser. Look at Shiloh, everybody! He's just like a worm," said Logan.

At this point, other students gathered around the fight, cheering Logan on. The school sure loved a good fight. And Logan would start one with a different student, it seemed, every month, so this was an event everyone seemed to anticipate with glee. Everyone except Shiloh and Emma. Speaking of her, the tenacious and vibrant girl that didn't look forward to these "barbaric events," as she called them, was cutting her way through the crowd of students like a fiery blade through butter.

Logan had pulled a jar of worms out of his backpack for this planned attack and was on top of Shiloh, dangling a slimy, wet worm no more than two or three inches away from his face.

"Look, worm! Look into the mirror," screamed Logan.

"Stop fighting, you two! You both are just embarrassing and completely barbaric. I refuse to believe we're in the same grade," Emma exclaimed.

Both boys had forgotten about each other entirely at this point and were staring at her, confused. Shiloh was confused because, to him, he had nothing to do with starting the fight. One thing was for sure, though. These boys both had a crush on Emma, but neither would admit it to themselves. In this brief moment of confusion, the worm in Logan's hand slipped away from his grip and dug itself into the ground.

The two boys got up and dusted themselves off. "I'm sorry. You're right. This is completely embarrassing," admitted Logan.

Whether his intentions were true was unclear. Was he going to flip the switch after this moment, or was he telling her what she wanted to hear? Shiloh just stared at the ground, avoiding Emma's gaze as she looked at him with concern. The bell rang, and it was off to their last classes of the day.

Shiloh was waiting in the front of the school for his grandma to pick him up, whom he was nervous to see because she would notice his bruises and the crust of dried blood under his nose. Shiloh saw Logan in his peripheral vision holding up a middle finger to him as he rode home on his bike.

Once Shiloh got home, he dashed up to his room and locked the door. Lucious, an old Siamese cat his grandparents had always had, let out a massive yawn after lying on his bed for hours as cats do. Shiloh sat down and started to weep, only to hear his grandma crying in her room, as well. The sound carried through the vents, almost as if a dying mouse were taking its last breaths. Shiloh knew she missed his grandfather, and so did he—almost as much as he missed his parents—but there was no coming back for them.

25

Chapter 2
Photos or Windows?

The next day was full of boring lessons that seemed pointless, or at least the three of them thought so. Logan could barely keep his eyes open during science class. He was bored to the point of exhaustion, yet he had them open just enough to peer over his shoulder at Shiloh's answers for today's quiz.

Once the lesson was over, it was finally time for lunch. Emma was starving. Her mom had packed her a lunch box like she did every day. Always the same things, too: a salami sandwich, a bag of pretzels, and a green apple. She bought water bottles from the vending machine to go with her lunch every day.

Logan saw her and decided to jog over a bit differently than he did yesterday.

"Hey, Emma. I just wanted to say sorry for yesterday. You know, the whole thing with Shiloh. I hope you don't think I'm some big jerk."

"If you're sorry, then don't apologize to me."

Logan looked puzzled. "What do you mean?"

She knocked him on the forehead with her knuckle and said, "If you're sorry, then apologize to Shiloh, not me, dummy!"

He scoffed. "That's what you'd like, isn't it? You've always had a soft spot for him."

"I don't know what your deal is, Logan, but you didn't use to be like this. We used to have playdates together as kids, don't you remember? Playing pretend and not having a care in the world?"

Logan was staring at his shoes at this, but nodded in agreement .

"Look, I miss that, Logan. This tough-guy thing you've got going on isn't you. If you want to join me, I'm going to find Shiloh," said Emma as she walked through him, bumping shoulders to assert her dominance.

However, seconds later, there was loud screaming. Logan fell to his knees.

Could the sound have been him? thought Emma, confused.

Logan felt his heart sink hearing all this, but the pain in his shoulder made him drop his tough-guy facade. Logan lifted his sleeve to reveal his shoulder. It looked horrible. Hundreds of cigarette burns had roughened his skin. The reason behind the burns was as sad as it was irritating. Logan's mom was an alcoholic. Her addiction started after her second attempt at birth, two years after Logan had been born. Her child was stillborn, and since receiving the news, she had become a shadow of herself. Everything was different from that moment on. On too many nights, she would get so intoxicated that she would end up going into Logan's room and putting her cigarettes out on him.

"I'm so sorry, Logan, I didn't know. How did you… It couldn't be your dad. He's a sweetheart! Oh my god, Logan… Did… your mom do this to you?" said Emma, after realizing the gravity of the situation.

Logan pulled down his sleeve. "It's fine. I'm fine."

Emma walked up to him and gave him a much-needed hug. "No, you're not, but it's okay. I'm here for you, bud," said Emma.

Logan sat there absorbing the feeling of feminine appreciation as he realized he had been "different" after being so neglected, and he thought maybe he could choose whom he let it out on. It wouldn't have to be the people he wanted around him, like Emma or even Shiloh.

The two children walked around the school campus looking for Shiloh in the library. This was a place Logan didn't visit very often, but he thought it was pretty cool because they had skateboarding magazines.

"Woah, Shiloh. Not looking to curse me after yesterday, are you? I'm sorry, okay?" said Logan, worried about the books Shiloh had checked out, which all seemed to be about magic, spells, the occult, and such.

Emma threw him a stern look.

Logan sighed, then said, "Look, I'm sorry for being a jerk. I honestly don't hate you or think you're a worm or whatever. Okay?"

Now it was Shiloh's turn to be confused. Logan had always been rude to him for as long as they'd known each other, but either way, it felt good to get the apology he had wanted all along.

"It's no worries, bro," said Shiloh.

Emma was happy they had made up. "I am stuck with the weirdest friends, aren't I?" she said to them both.

"Friends?" the boys asked in unison, not sure if they'd heard her correctly.

"But seriously, Shiloh, what in God's name are you reading?" Emma asked.

Yet perhaps even more intriguing, why would a school have books on magic and the occult?

The school's librarian was Ms. Fiera, a twenty-eight-year-old brunette with wide, green eyes and glasses that sat on top of her average-sized nose. Most of the teachers and even a few of the students had a crush on her. She regularly studied Wicca and practiced magic in her garden in her spare time. She always picked up new books every time she visited a local occult bookshop on the main street in town. More so, the librarian enjoyed reading while working and would often mix up her Wiccan literature with other books from the library. Inevitably, they would simply get lost in the mix and, in turn, be put into the school's rotation of reading material. To her advantage, however, the school's dean, Mr. Dobbs, didn't care as much for the school's library as he did for the sports division. He was a huge basketball fan, and he rarely paid attention to the requests made by Ms. Fiera for new books. Maybe if he had, she'd not be working there on account that he'd pay more attention to the literature being distributed to the children.

Ms. Fiera's inability to maintain possession of her idealistic literature meant that these three students were in for more than they had bargained for.

"I was hoping to find something… about my grandpa," said Shiloh. "I don't know why. I just… I hate… hearing my grandma cry every night, and I… it's just been a lot to handle, so… I understand if… you guys don't want to be friends with a loser like me."

Logan and Emma looked at him with serious faces.

"We're not going anywhere," assured Emma. She was now staring at him with her hand on his shoulder as he looked up at her. Emma then looked deeply into his eyes and saw the tears coming out. She was concerned for her friend, yes, but she could also feel Shiloh's pain. Her parents had always been absent: her dad always working and never being home, and her mom always working at home but never paying attention. She missed the days with her parents before things changed and everything got more… exhausting. Looking into Shiloh's eyes for a good four or five seconds, she saw in him the same pain she felt, and it more than assured her that she wanted nothing but to stand by him and be there, in a way others just couldn't or didn't want to understand.

Logan didn't say anything, but he walked up to Shiloh and hugged him. He could see that he wasn't the only person hurting, and even though his pain was valid in every way, it didn't make everybody else's problems disappear. Logan recognized some of his pain in Shiloh as well. Not a pain caused by missing somebody, but a pain caused by the people you love intending to hurt you.

This hug went on for a few seconds until Emma sighed and shouted, "ALRIGHT, it's a group hug!"

The three all felt a sense of belonging in this moment. It was a feeling they hadn't got to experience in a long time: family.

The children quickly wiped their tears and got back to the topic at hand.

"What the hell are you reading, bro?" asked Logan, looking seriously concerned at this point.

Shiloh replied, "Well, in an unlucky attempt to find any clue whatsoever to where my grandpa might have disappeared to, I grabbed a few of the witchy-looking books on Ms. Fiera's desk."

Emma was surprised and a little angry as she exclaimed, "Shiloh, why would you do such a STUPID thing? I mean, not looking for your Grandpa! But… stealing the books from Ms. Fiera?"

He knew this was coming, but already had a response. "Look, I'm going to put it back once I leave, okay? I wasn't going to steal it. It's just… borrowing. Plus, I don't know. I just thought anything was better than nothing."

Emma could see his point. If it were her grandfather, she'd do anything to save him, too. "Alright, so if we're going to be reading for lunch, we might as well all grab some books, I think."

They went off to find books to read. Meanwhile, Shiloh was dedicated to finding anything to lead him closer to his grandfather, Everett.

"There's got to be something," mumbled Shiloh under his breath. Flipping through the pages of *In the Desert Is an Ocean*, an occult book of Ms. Fiera's about white magic and nature spells, Shiloh was hoping to find more besides clues that could lead him to his grandfather. Since he was a kid, he had stared at spoons and crayons for moments at a time, trying to bend and move them with his mind, which always ended up in him giving up and wishing he had superpowers. In a way, Shiloh craved any type of power at all. He had lost his parents and now his grandfather, and whether he wanted it to or not, it was also affecting his grandma. Shiloh could use anything to take more control of his situation. At this point, he just felt hopeless. Admittedly, though, Shiloh felt a huge weight lift off his shoulders with his new friends in the picture.

Emma walked back up to their table with a handful of books. She showed them to Shiloh and said, "I found a book by my mom. I didn't know the school had any copies of her work."

Shiloh grabbed it and smirked. He loved Emma's mom's books. His grandfather used to read them to him every time his family let him visit his grandparents' house.

"I also grabbed this because it reminded me of your dad. I thought it'd be interesting," said Emma, handing a book titled *Carpentry 101* to Logan.

"Why would you get me this?" complained Logan.

He didn't much care for carpentry. After all, it was the passion that left his father so distracted that he still hadn't noticed Logan's shoulder burns.

"I've seen cooler professions, that's for sure," said Logan, wanting to end the conversation and the book that started it out of sight.

Shiloh and Emma both noticed his tone, so they tried to turn his attention to something else.

"What else did you find?" asked Emma, who was mostly just interested in learning more about Logan's preferred style of literature.

"I just grabbed it off of Ms. Fiera's desk because it looked old as hell, and I was bored, but then as I opened it, I noticed a name on the list of people that checked it out in the past," said Logan.

"And?" asked Emma. "What is it?"

Shiloh looked up at Logan, realizing that a clue might have been found.

"What did you find, Logan?" asked Shiloh.

"Well... look," said Logan as he handed Shiloh an old, deteriorating stack of pages.

Shiloh saw the name "Seven Evans" written in green ink under the list of people that had previously checked out the old book. Shiloh's grandfather had this nickname because, for reasons unknown, Everett only had seven fingers.

Shiloh's stomach filled with excitement. "GUYS! Do you know what this means? My grandpa somehow must've checked this book out... but he is too old? How did he manage that?"

"Well," Emma added, "I wonder if Ms. Fiera's books have been getting mixed up with the rest because if so, then maybe she knows your grandpa."

"There's no way. He was too old. How would he know her? She's like…" Shiloh paused.

"Hot," blurted Logan.

Emma rolled her eyes. "Ugh, come on, guys."

As Logan defended his stance on the matter, Shiloh looked deeper into the book his grandfather's name was written on. Flipping through the pages, he noticed all sorts of black ink smears and page tears over what seemed to be runic symbols he hadn't seen before, along with little illustrations and commentaries. One page, in particular, caught his eye. It was probably because of the comments written in red ink rather than black, making him look twice. It seemed rather peculiar to him.

This page featured an illustration of a table that looked strangely familiar to Shiloh.

"Do you guys know what kind of book this is?" asked Shiloh, handing it over to them. They looked it over together for a while and then on their own for a little longer, until they came to a similar conclusion.

"Well, it looks creepy, and maybe we shouldn't be messing with something this old. Ms. Fiera would tan our hides if she found out we were 'borrowing' reading materials from her," said Emma.

"Yeah, I mean, if I had to guess, I'd say this looks like the opposite of a bible," said Logan jokingly.

Shiloh still couldn't tell where he'd seen the table before, the thought refusing to leave his mind.

"You could ask your grandma," said Emma, "because maybe she'll know if he checked it out and all, and also, she probably would've seen him reading it, right?"

All of a sudden, it all made sense to Shiloh. "I don't think we'll have to."

The other two looked at him like he was crazy.

Logan, who was particularly concerned and trying to be motivational for once, said, "Come on, man, you can't give up that easily!"

Shiloh looked up at them. "No, you don't understand, and… that's okay. I'll explain everything later. Just… meet me at my house around eleven tonight, and you'll see what I mean, I promise."

The bell rang, and Emma and Logan watched Shiloh run off to class, confused but in agreement that they would be at Shiloh's house later that night.

Chapter 3

Breaking the Rules

Tonight wasn't the first time Emma had snuck out. She would often do it on the nights her dad was away on work trips. Not that her mother would have let her go out at night. Or at least not intentionally. C. J. always seemed to prioritize her writing over anything else, and Emma no longer felt as "connected" to her mother as she used to. On the upside, though, Emma could easily sneak out of the house as she pleased. She often did it to see if her mom would notice, and when she wouldn't, Emma would climb onto the roof at night and watch the stars.

"The stars look crazy tonight, don't they," Logan asked Emma.

They both were on their way to Shiloh's house. Emma looked up, and to her surprise, the stars were plentiful. Her gaze switched to Logan, who was also gazing at the sky. She began to notice things about him she rarely saw in school. His head looked bare, like he had just had a fresh haircut. The sides of his head were shaved clean, yet he kept the top entirely covered in thick, lengthy hair combed over to the side. His joggers and shirt were black, and his sleeves were ripped off, showing just a bit of his young but athletic physique. She was excited about what the night might bring. They both were catching their breaths when Logan checked his phone for the time.

"It's ten fifty-eight."

"Right on time," Emma chimed in.

They smiled at each other and then set their bikes against the short, white fence surrounding the curious tiny house.

The lights were all off, except for the reading light Shiloh's grandma had left on by her bedside. The kids could almost make out her sleeping figure.

Noticing the time, Shiloh hurried downstairs and opened the front door. He noticed Logan and Emma at the front gate, just as he had hoped. He wasn't sure whether they would show up or not, but seeing them there made Shiloh remember Emma's words from earlier: *We're not going anywhere.* He left the door cracked, walked over to the gate, and unlocked it.

"Dude, you'd swear this is like a Keebler elf cottage or something," Logan whispered, trying to hold back his laughter.

"I can't believe you guys came," said Shiloh.

"Obviously," said Emma. "You can't just talk us up and not come clean about whatever you were supposed to tell us!"

Shiloh realized his friends were there because he was supposed to tell them the truth about his discovery the other day.

"Follow me, but be quiet. My grandma is an extremely light sleeper, and the halls here creak like frogs."

Logan was about to start laughing again; his face was so red. Yet seeing Shiloh's expression, he cleared his throat, brushed himself off, and quickly regained his composure, remembering this was a serious matter. Emma also gave Shiloh a nod, and the children followed him from the yard through the house and downstairs, into the basement.

Shiloh shut the door behind them and turned to look at his friends.

"This, this is the table in that book we found!" Logan exclaimed.

"Shiloh, what does this mean? Why is this table here and in the book? Do you think your grandpa could've used a spell or something from that page we saw?" asked Emma.

Shiloh wasn't too surprised that Emma had turned out to be as perceptive as always. After all, she was the smartest girl he knew.

"Bingo," said Shiloh in a raspy voice, a grin growing on his face. "I think, somehow… this table and this book have something to do with my grandpa's disappearance."

Logan didn't like where this was going. "What? Do you seriously want us to believe your grandpa did some voodoo magic spell and disappeared? No, Shiloh, there has to be an explanation for everything. Things don't just happen *magically*."

Emma put her hand on Logan's shoulder, which wasn't covered in fresh burn wounds, and brought her face close to his. The girl's gesture sent a tingling sensation up his spine that he had never felt before.

"Yes, they do," she whispered.

Logan realized what she meant. He thought it wasn't fair to say everything was rational when he couldn't rationalize his mom's actions. Shiloh was sitting in his grandfather's office chair. It was an aged leather that you could smell as you sat on it. Shiloh enjoyed this smell and spun around a few times in it before turning to his friends again.

"So, guys, what if the book and the table work together and it's supposed to show us something or bring him back or who knows?!"

Emma walked over to the table and ran her fingers across the dips of the runes carved into it. The intricate details were truly mesmerizing. Logan followed her, but was more reluctant because of his distaste for carpentry and most things that reminded him of his dad.

"Is it just me, or do the symbols on this table look a lot like the ones in here?" said Logan while skimming through the ancient book.

"You're right. The symbols in the book are identical to the carvings on the table, but I have no clue what they mean," said Emma.

They were close but still nowhere near a satisfying conclusion. What did the symbols mean?

The children started investigating more of the items scattered on the floor next to them. Dusty, old books were stacked in piles around the table, along with a house blueprint that neither of the children recognized. Beneath the blueprint, the children also found a brass compass.

Logan puffed over the pile of dusty books, trying to reveal their spines, but only ended up getting the dust in Shiloh's eyes.

"Ow, was that really necessary, Logan?" said Shiloh.

"Yes, it was. Emma, look! Aren't these some of your mom's books?" asked Logan.

Emma walked up to the boys, her mouth agape. "Why would those be here?"

Shiloh stopped spinning and got out of his grandfather's leather chair. "Look, this is going to sound cheesy, but my grandpa used to read me those as a kid. We loved them. I used to make him read *Starsurfers* all the time because I would have the trippiest dreams after hearing it and, oh yeah! That book on Atlantis about the last day of their civilization, like WHAT the… and yeah… I don't know. He and I liked your mom's work."

This whole time, Logan had a smile on his face, probably relieved that it wasn't him who was put on blast for his love of children's books.

Emma was flattered. She realized how incredibly influential her mom's books must've been.

"I'm happy my mom was able to make your childhood a little more interesting. That's crazy. I didn't think that many people read them. I haven't even read much of them myself. I hate how much she works. It creates a space between us. She loves her work, you know, more than me, I guess," Emma said then broke down in tears.

The two boys looked at each other, confused about how to make her feel better.

Shiloh went over to the pile of books that Emma's mom wrote, dusted them with his shirt, and handed them to her.

"I'm sorry. I feel stupid," Emma said as she wiped her eyes.

"You're not. You're one of the coolest people I know, Emma, seriously. And not only that, you have a cool mom who loves you. You have no idea how jealous I am of you," said Shiloh.

Emma noticed the look in his eyes and could tell he wished he still had his mom. She took the books from his grasp and put them in her bag.

"Thank you, Shiloh," she said before grabbing his shirt and pulling him in for a hug.

Logan felt a bit jealous. After all, he thought that maybe since she knew about his situation at home, there might've been more between them, but he tried to shake off the feelings and tell himself it would be stupid to like her anyway, and he almost believed it.

The three children gathered around the tome, with questions racing in their minds, one after the other. They were intrigued and knew what they were dealing with was nothing short of significant. How could a book this old still hold itself together? What did Shiloh's grandfather have to do with all of this? Where was he? They didn't even know where to start.

Emma looked at the book's page with the table on it, which had fallen out at this point. She noticed something peculiar on the page next to some symbols they could not decipher. It seemed to be a familiar yet foreign language.

"Hey, guys… I think I found something weird, and I think it's Latin, but I could be wrong," said Emma.

Shiloh walked around the table to inspect her findings.

Meanwhile, Logan was under the table eating some cookies he'd found in the kitchen on the way down that he snuck into his trousers.

Hearing the crunching noises from below, Emma popped her head under the table.

"Logan, you're unbelievable," she said, as she snatched the cookie right out of his hand and took a bite out of it before tossing it across the room and into the trash can.

"Gee, thanks, Emma. My low blood sugar is super thankful. I could die, you know," said Logan.

Emma ignored him and continued her transcription of the foreign language.

Logan dusted the crumbs off of his shoes under the table and accidentally hit his head.

"Ow, what the—"

Looking up, he noticed a black stamp on the wood with a signature that looked familiar.

"Why, though…" Logan wondered.

How could his father be wrapped up in all of this?

"Guys, my dad made this table. Come look. Right here is his stamp! I don't know if tonight is just some big intertwining of random events or if everything happens for a reason. But I think things are starting to feel a bit freakier."

The other two climbed under the table to verify if Logan had found another clue. Emma pulled out her flashlight to see it, and there it was: the familiar signature stamp Logan's father would put on all his custom-made products from the store.

"You know, Shiloh," said Emma, "I'm starting to think Logan's right. Things feel weird."

She looked down and noticed the phrase she had mentioned before, which she suspected might be of Latin origin. She pointed it out to the other two, and they each took turns trying to pronounce it. They felt it was the least they could do, seeing that the transcription was somewhat readable compared to the torn book pages. The first few rounds of pronunciations had the group cracking smiles until after Emma had given it a try, and Shiloh had an odd feeling of déjà vu upon hearing it. Like a camera shutter closing and capturing its subject, Shiloh's mind clicked, and he remembered where he'd heard the saying before.

Before his grandfather, Everett, disappeared, Shiloh used to stay up well past his bedtime playing video games. When taking his restroom breaks in the bathroom down the hall, the boy would often hear the muffled sounds of his grandfather yelling from his study.

"That's it! Sometimes, I heard him screaming THIS from the basement at night," said Shiloh, convinced that each new clue led them closer to finding his grandfather. "But you're saying one part of it wrong." "Let's keep in mind, though, that the man you heard saying this gibberish disappeared into thin air, so maybe we first need to decide IF we should say it or not," said Logan.

Shiloh knew Logan was right. They needed to be cautious if they were going to bring his grandfather back. As bad as he wanted to see him again, they couldn't afford to mess anything up. Yet, fate was on their side that night. They all sat in silence for a moment as they imagined all the possibilities of the incantation.

After a moment, though, Emma grew impatient. "What's the worst that could happen? It's just words. After all, I want to know where I messed up the pronunciation."

Though unsure at first, Logan felt he, too, had not much to lose from a few words scribbled in a dusty old book.

Remembering the incantation his grandfather always used to say, Shiloh closed his eyes and whispered, *"Quod est superius est sicut quod inferius."*

No later than the words left Shiloh's lips, the children felt a chill filling the basement. They noticed a cool, white glow by the table on the other side of the room. As they walked around it, they saw the light was coming from the runes etched into the wooden surface.

"OKAY, THIS IS… GUYS, THE TABLE IS… YOU SEE THIS, RIGHT?" shrieked Logan, unsettled.

The table then began to hover a few centimeters above the ground, spinning slowly. It emanated a low-frequency humming that resembled a feeling of warmth the closer the children got to it.

"Is… is this what magic feels like?" asked Emma.

As the table slowly rotated between the children, the books and trinkets piled on top of it fell off, leaving fewer things littering the table and allowing more light to seep through the exposed symbols.

The old tome the three friends had found in the library now had smoke coming out of it, filling the room and making them cough.

"WHAT'S GOING ON?" screamed Logan.

"I don't know but look at the book! It's on fire," replied Shiloh, much calmer than his friend.

In a matter of seconds, the book was gone. All that was left was a pile of dust that wafted away shortly after its combustion. The three of them looked up, yet couldn't figure out what to say. They had just seen a book incinerate itself and were now staring at a floating, glowing table. This evening was officially far from ordinary.

How Shiloh's grandma hadn't woken up from the noise, they did not know but also didn't question. The three children were bewildered at what was going on, and undoubtedly felt drawn to the table, as if the humming was somehow speaking to them and suggesting they get closer.

Logan looked up at his friends as they both raised their hands over the table, so he did the same.

"Don't look back," said Shiloh.

The children closed in; palms firmly pressed on its trembling surface. It felt intoxicating for a few seconds, then nothing. None of them could see or hear anything.

Yet one thing was certain: They were no longer in Shiloh's basement.

Chapter 4

The Fisherman With No Bait

One after the other, the children opened their eyes. They were immediately blinded by how bright it was. It was like being woken up by sunlight. It was a beautifully innocent scene as they woke up a few feet apart on a wet, sandy shore.

Emma, Logan, and Shiloh got up, brushed the sand off of their clothes, and looked around in awe. They woke up on a beach, yet how they got there was a mystery. After brushing themselves off, they slowly turned their gaze to one another, wondering who would be the first to speak.

"How did... what... just happened?" asked Emma.

The sky was bright, and with the sun's location overhead, it seemed to be around noon. There were no seagulls or anything on the beach that they could see. Nothing besides themselves, the sand, and the ocean. It smelled delicious, too, like a gust through a window left open on a rainy day mixed with the ocean's refreshing, salty breeze. Shiloh thought it was peculiar that there were no birds around because back when his family visited the beach, one of his favorite things was to feed the seagulls.

"Something feels off," said Shiloh. "There are no birds or anything. We're alone … completely off the grid."

Logan turned to see his bag lying on the ground a few meters away. Emma noticed him grab it and then saw hers, so she followed his lead and did the same. In his backpack was a pack of cigarettes that he would carry around, a lighter, and a jar of worms—the same pot he had in the schoolyard a few days ago. He was curious why his bag had followed him here.

Emma wondered the same as she opened up hers. Inside were the few books her mom wrote, along with a few other books and small items. Realizing this, Emma traced the events back to before they had been transported here by some unknown power.

"THE TABLE! You guys remember it, right? How we got here?" said Emma, trying to see if her friends had reached the same conclusion.

Seconds passed, and they started to remember the basement, the table, the strange incantation, and the glowing runes. The incantation that made the table glow as if by magic was still stuck in their minds. After all, how could they possibly forget after having been transported somewhere else by four seemingly innocuous little words?

"I knew something magical was going to happen. I'm just... a little foggy on why we would end up at a beach," replied Shiloh.

The children wandered along the shore for what felt like a few hours. It was the most beautiful day out as it went on. A light breeze from the waves kept the children feeling refreshed enough to walk through the warm, sandy dunes, looking for a clue as to why they were there. Logan distanced himself from the group by a few feet as the other two walked on next to each other. He was feeling bewildered by the whole experience, so he wasn't saying much. Emma, who was very good at being empathic with the two boys, noticed this and slowed down to meet Logan's pace. She was concerned, as any good friend should be.

"What's wrong, Logan?"

He turned his head away from the waves to look at her. "It's like... okay... I get how we got here and why we're doing this... but part of me is... nervous, I guess, to be so far from home and somewhere out here in the middle of nowhere. I'm not trying to get lost, and it's not like I'm scared, but how did we end up on a beach, and how can I know that this is real, and not some... dream?"

Emma resonated with how Logan felt. It was scary being so uncertain of your next move. In an attempt to comfort her friend, she leaned over to him and kissed him on the cheek. This made Logan stop walking and look up at her with a face that was now glowing red with embarrassment. Logan had a weird feeling in his stomach, similar to when Emma leaned in close to him at Shiloh's place before this whole insane endeavor. Accurate or not, this was the reality Logan wanted to be authentic. He felt much better and continued walking with a bit more purpose in his step.

Shiloh didn't know how he felt for a minute. Walking beside Emma, he fell silent and stared ahead, not too concerned with her presence. If what he'd just heard happen behind him did indeed happen, then he would be an idiot to still have a crush on her.

"Everything okay?" asked Emma.

Shiloh looked at her with a half-smile. "All good."

As he continued to focus ahead to avoid another awkward silence, Shiloh noticed a figure ahead on the shore. The figure was blurry, but as they approached, it became clearer what it was. It was a man fishing. He was wearing a pair of yellow rubber overalls that kept his body dry as he fished—at least for the most part, as he was knee-deep in the water, casting his line out over and over.

The children stopped in their tracks, trying to decide their next move.

"We should avoid him. What if he tries to hurt us?" said Logan, concerned mainly for his safety.

"What's he going to do, nick you with his fish hook? He doesn't look like Indiana Jones," replied Shiloh. "Wait… where's Emma?"

The boys turned their attention to Emma, who was now only inches away from the fisherman.

"What is she doing?" Logan exclaimed.

"She's going to get herself hurt," replied Shiloh.

The boys ran after her but were too late to stop their friend.

"EXCUSE ME! Would you happen to know where we are? My name is Emma, and these are my friends, and … we're lost," Emma shouted in a sweet but well-projected tone.

The fisherman looked at her for a second and then cast his hook into the water again as if he couldn't understand her. He reeled his line back in, and Logan noticed he didn't have anything but a weight on his hook. There was no bait at all. The children saw this and thought it was peculiar, but it seemed to have irked Logan more than the others. Logan usually went fishing with his dad, who would always set him up with a rod and let the boy pick out the bait. This caught Logan by surprise, and he wondered why anybody would fish without bait.

Logan looked in his bag and, after a moment of contemplation, pulled out his jar of worms. He walked up and tapped the fisherman on the arm, who then turned to him. Logan went on and showed him the jar of worms. When the fisherman noticed what he was being offered, he returned his attention to casting and reeling his line, not paying the boy any mind. Logan went back his friends, who were watching the scene unfold.

This place felt familiar to them all, yet they did not know why.

"Are we in a different country or reality or something?" asked Shiloh.

"Seems so. But wherever we are, is there food around? Because starvation is not exactly how I intend on going out," replied Logan.

They all brainstormed their best next move and agreed it would be worth a shot to ask the fisherman for directions or guidance of any sort, since he was the only person they had seen on the beach the entire day.

As the group once again approached the fisherman, Logan took a step forward to be the one to talk to him again. He figured that if they were going to find Shiloh's grandfather and get out of there, walking in circles all day wouldn't do them any good. Yet what caught him by surprise this time was the massive pile of dead fish next to the pole Logan had not noticed before.

"How did… you catch…"

Logan composed himself and looked the fisherman dead in the eyes, which he noticed were brown and welcoming.

"WE NEED TO GET HOME!" shouted the boy.

Startled, the fisherman dropped his rod in the water, which oddly sank and disappeared. The children gazed at the man as he turned to face Logan, worried about what he might do. He then began running toward the boy alarmingly fast.

"LOGAN, RUN!" yelled Emma and Shiloh.

Logan closed his eyes and didn't move an inch. He was frozen with fear. As the fisherman collided with the boy, he turned to sand and collapsed in the rest of the dunes.

Logan remained unmoving. He opened his eyes, and the other two ran up to greet him with a hug. Shiloh noticed that the pile of fish caught by the man was slowly starting to move. This gave Shiloh a feeling of déjà vu. Yet there was no way he would have experienced this before. The fish continued moving more and more until they were animated enough to flop themselves back into the ocean.

After witnessing this unusual episode, the children saw the reflective scales return to the surface, along with the silhouette of an object they seemed to be pushing. The fish were working together to push what they recognized as the carved magic table ashore.

As the sun went down, the three friends were still trying to figure out what to do next. Logan placed his hand on the table, which made the other two nervous.

"Logan, don't," insisted Shiloh.

"Yeah, you don't know how it works. You could get us all killed," said Emma.

"And… you think you do?" asked Logan, in a tone that caught Emma by surprise.

"Yes, I think I might have an idea."

"Let's hear it then!"

Emma pulled out a book from her bag. It was one that her mother had written.

"I think we're inside my mom's book."

Hearing herself say this made Emma feel better about her mother. After all, the day was beautiful, and if her mother could create that with her writing, it was certainly a worthwhile pursuit.

No matter how stupid it sounded at first, this possibility made complete sense in Logan and Shiloh's minds.

"Are we in…" started Shiloh, already knowing the answer.

"Yup," responded Emma. "We're in *The Fisherman with No Bait.*"

The children plopped down in the soft, warm dunes. It was getting colder, as the sun had been down for nearly an hour.

"So we can't get back home because there's no book about home?" asked Logan.

"Only thing I'm pretty sure of," said Emma, "is that we can go into the books we have."

Emma's bag wasn't huge, but it weighed a lot. She pulled out another book from her bag.

"Ah, a classic," said Shiloh. "My mom would read me *Starsurfers* all the time as a kid, but one night I had these weird nightmares that I was falling into the sun, like in the story. After that, I stopped asking her to read it to me."

He handed the novel over to Logan. "Are there any space diners we can visit in it, or is it just wishful thinking?

I've never read this one."

Emma grabbed the book from Logan's hands, walked over, and placed it on the table. "Put your hands over the table. We have to touch it at the same time, I think."

It made sense to the boys, so they did what she asked.

"Okay but hold up. If we're really going to keep going on and stuff and… like… looking for Shiloh's grandpa, we need an escape plan, too. Otherwise, how are we supposed to save him or ourselves?" interrupted Logan.

He had a point. Shiloh wanted to save his grandfather just as much as Emma wanted to discover more about her mom and how she felt about her writing. No doubt they were meddling with powers that could destroy just as much as create.

"Obviously, this table is some kind of old magic," said Emma. "There was a book that might've given us more clues, but unfortunately, that's no longer an option as it burst into flames. So, if any of us get split up, the other two should look for the one missing. We aren't leaving anybody behind."

The children agreed, though Shiloh still had a few questions.

"How do you think we are supposed to find the table, though? This one was submerged in the ocean! It could be impossible to find it," said Shiloh.

"Logan, what do you think?" asked Emma.

She noticed he was biting his thumbnail and staring off past them, deep in thought.

"Well," said Logan, "I think that somehow, we willed the table to show itself to us. Look at the fisherman. We asked him to leave, and doing so made the table reveal itself."

The other two realized Logan was actually onto something.

"So what you're saying is that, when we go into the next book, the table will try to reveal itself?" asked Emma.

"I think so. I have no clue for sure, but I mean, come on! It makes sense, right?"

It made perfect sense to the children. So they pledged not to leave each other behind as they went forward, knowing that somehow, they would have to locate the table, which would reveal itself at some point. The question still on their mind was how, but they could only discover that on the other side.

Eager to embark on their next adventure, the children gathered closer to the table. They laid their right hands on the wooden surface while focusing on the book that sat in the middle. It was a copy of *Starsurfers.* Looking at each other, they each gave a nod. Logan closed his eyes because, though they were all incredibly nervous about what was to come, he was also feeling a bit nauseous. Shiloh and Emma also closed their eyes, preparing themselves for the giant leap they were about to make.

"Three… two… one…" Emma counted down, eager to participate in what seemed to have become a ritual.

After that first experience, the children knew how magic worked and never forgot those hollow but powerful words that made it all happen. Shiloh opened his eyes and, as they stared at the table with eyes full of intent, they all spoke the incantation in unison, *"Quod est superius est sicut quod inferius!"*

Though the children had no idea what the words meant, it didn't matter. They were off, traveling into Emma's mom's book, *Starsurfers.*

All that was left on the shore was the splash of water that had once formed the table. It had collapsed into the waves once again, rejoining the larger body rolling in and out of the bay. The days continued here, dream-like and infinite. Meanwhile, the children were about to wake up in what seemed like another dream.

Chapter 5

Play Your Role

These glimpses of time in between their destinations felt as if they were immediately put to sleep, though they had little time for dreams. As the three children started to come their senses again, they found themselves on a cold, glass-like surface that was pitch black and shiny, enough so they could see their reflections. White spots were reflecting from behind them, they noticed, which caused them to look up and see a vast network of stars covering up the infinity of the night sky. They were floating in space, and it seemed endless. There was also a lot of noise from what sounded like machines of sorts powering this active yet barren planet.

Shiloh stood up, looked over at his friends who were gathering themselves, and remembered why he was there. He wasn't sure if the others did, though. It was almost as if they all lost their memory a bit each time the table would take them places.

"What happened?" asked Emma curiously.

Logan nodded in agreement as they both looked at Shiloh. He was twiddling his fingers as if trying to concoct a grand plan in his head.

"I'm not sure, but wherever we are, we are alone," Shiloh replied.

The children set out to explore this dark planet for a while, hearing plenty of noises but not locating them. A few minutes in, Emma noticed her mother's book, *Starsurfers*, lying on the ground and picked it up without mentioning it to the boys. This likely meant that the table might not be too much further, so she pressed on. After walking a few miles, however, a high-pitched ringing noise pierced the darkness, even louder than the original low humming that the planet seemed to have been emitting "naturally."

Further ahead and seemingly unbothered by the sudden commotion, Logan was kicking rocks, trying to pass the time. One of the rocks, however, caught him off guard. It didn't move when he kicked it; rather, it sank into the ground and disappeared.

Then, out of nowhere, appeared a black metal staircase leading down into a hole in the ground, the end of which was not visible to their eyes.

"You're wrong if you think I'm going down there," said Logan.

Shiloh chuckled. It wasn't any surprise his friend was at his wits' end because he was, too.

Emma poked Logan in the arm and said, "Look, I don't know what else there is to do, so we might as well. We won't get out of here or find Seven Eva…

Excuse me, Shiloh's grandpa any sooner unless we investigate this."

Shiloh smiled. He thought it was cute, though he didn't like it as much when others said it. Emma looked embarrassed, but it had come out only because that was what she would call him before realizing how great of a man Everett was.

"She's right," Shiloh said. "The only way out is forward."

Shiloh took the first steps down the clanking metal staircase, closely followed by the other two. The high-pitched noise grew louder as they descended for what seemed to be countless minutes. In fact, by this point, the whistle had become so sharp it was giving Emma a headache. Though their feet were getting sore, the children felt relieved to see a white door in the distance. Even more curious, this door also seemed to have been the source of the loud ringing filling their ears.

Though nervous about what may lie on the other side, Emma was keen on putting a stop to the ceaseless rattle, so she delivered a forceful kick to the door, blasting it open and leaving both boys with their jaws on the floor.

The sound, though muffled before, was now clear and oddly familiar. The children took steps forward onto a terrace with awe in their eyes as they looked upon a big city.

"Looks kind of like… New York," said Logan, though he had only really seen the metropolis online.

Still, that didn't mean the boy wasn't right. This city was highly reminiscent of New York, though instead of cars using fossil fuels for energy, the vehicles of this planet seemed to fly using a different power source. There was so much going on that the children could only stand there, transfixed, before anyone uttered a word.

Emma and Shiloh, on the other hand, were having a different experience. Since both of them still remembered the plot and setting of *Starsurfers*, they had a rough idea of what might await them in this world, unlike Logan. The two friends conversed about how they felt they were familiar with what they saw, a world beneath the surface—the surface being a solar panel and the civilization living underneath it in advanced technological towers spanning from the surface to the core. The habitable areas were protected from the core's heat, and they were also teeming with life. There were vehicles of different styles, all whirring up and down the city to a gentle, low hum. Personnel, who looked like ants from where the children stood, were diligently carrying out their duties to ensure the planet's progress. There wasn't anywhere habitable on this planet that wasn't already bustling with activity.

Though Emma and Shiloh were feeling more comfortable knowing where they were, Logan was not as hopeful. Shiloh began to map out their next move and explain how they would make their way down to a row of buildings just beyond the terrace. They were to look for a clue that his grandfather might've left.

Yet after a while, Logan stopped listening as his head filled with doubts about their plan.

"LOOK, we have no water, it's hot as hell, and we have no idea where the table is. I can only think the right thing to do right now would be to locate something to drink before we go off trying to do something we've got no energy for," the boy interjected.

Sweat was dripping down his brow as he shouted, not because he was angry, but because he was exhausted. Not only was his brain being pushed to its limits, but his body was catching up with it, too. Logan retracted after his outburst, leaning back onto the black wall behind the terrace in defeat.

Shiloh and Emma looked at each other, visibly concerned for their friend.

"Look, you're right. We need water if we're going to get any further," said Shiloh.

He then pulled out a mechanical pencil that he had in his pocket and walked over to Emma, whom he had noticed earlier had picked up the book.

"May I see that, please?" asked Shiloh, and the girl handed it over to him.

Shiloh opened the book to the very first pages that talked of a hollow planet lost among the vastness of stars. The very one they were on.

At the bottom of the page, Shiloh added the following with his mechanical pencil: "… *and the best part about this planet was that no matter where you went, there was always a snack vending machine close by.*"

He then closed the book and pressed his lips to it while the other two stared at him with curiosity.

"WHY WOULD YOU WRITE IN THE BOOK? I CAN'T BELIEVE— WHAT THE—" screamed Logan.

Yet as he turned around, Logan couldn't believe his eyes when he saw a vending machine stocked full of sodas, water bottles, snacks, and all sorts of goodies.

"Woah! Way to go, Shiloh!" said Emma, impressed with the boy's wit.

Logan was the first to the buttons, pounding in letters and numbers, plotting out how he would eat as many snacks as he could now that his parents weren't around to see him. Yet upon closer inspection, the boy's enthusiasm was tempered almost in an instant.

"Shiloh, you're a disappointment," said Logan, blandly.

Logan snatched the book and pencil out of Shiloh's hands and erased the period at the end of Shiloh's paragraph. Then he added something of his own: "*...and it didn't require any money.*"

Emma and Shiloh laughed while Logan pounded away at the vending machine again, eager to get the snacks he needed so badly.

In the meantime, Emma and Shiloh were lost in conversation. They discussed their memories of the book and its plot. *Starsurfers* was about a civilization of future humans that terraformed a dwarf star by building a shell around it that had the properties of a giant solar panel. While the two were talking, Logan looked at the book and flipped through the chapters, skimming through for even an ounce of insight into what this place would be like. Bits and pieces felt oddly familiar, while others felt foreign.

"I'm not sure exactly how this will play out, but we can't just sit here and wait for something to happen," Emma said.

The boys looked at each other and nodded in agreement, but they noticed a change in her facial expression when they returned their gaze to her.

"Emma, what's wrong?" asked Shiloh, concerned.

Emma looked nervous, but for a good reason. She had read her mother's book many times, and with this knowledge came a scary detail: Those who ruled the planet they were now on weren't exactly human.

"What do you think these people are? Aliens, or are they human like us?" asked Logan.

Emma was quick with her response. "They're supposedly 'future humans' whose primary focus is survival and who have discarded the need for emotions millions of years before. In other words, we couldn't have stumbled upon a more dangerous and volatile environment than this."

Shiloh and Logan both gulped upon hearing this. Though Shiloh would do anything to find his grandfather, it didn't mean he wasn't a little nervous. He was terrified, but knowing how far they'd come, he also didn't want all of their efforts to be for nothing.

A high-pitched sound from above alerted the children to a new presence. They looked up to see what looked like a UFO the size of a bus coming down, followed by two more. All three zoomed down and landed right in front of them. A few minutes passed, and the children stood there dumbfounded, just waiting to see what would happen next.

A door in one of the UFOs cracked open and let out a burst of smoke, out of which emerged several human-like figures dressed in what seemed to be military clothing. Their skin was translucent, gray, and transparent. They had a type of intricate technology inside them that was visible under their skin and brains where their heads were supposed to be. They did not need lungs, a heart, or any other organs, for that matter. They solely needed a brain to function and did not experience any emotions whatsoever, so, to the children, they were robotic.

More personnel swarmed the perimeter soon after, preventing the children from devising an escape plan. They were surrounded with no means of escape.

"Shiloh, the book!" shouted Emma.

Shiloh grabbed it from Logan's waistline and immediately handed it to Emma.

"The pencil, who has the— NO! GET OFF OF ME!" she screamed.

The robots grabbed the book from her hands, preventing Shiloh from handing the pencil to Emma in time. The robots then seized the children, who were unable to break through their tight grasp.

"You are under arrest for trespassing on private property," said the robot personnel all at once.

"GIVE ME MY BOOK BACK! THAT IS NOT YOURS TO TAKE!" Emma screamed back at them.

Once again, the robots replied in unison, "Items and substances of any matter are not permitted on private property here on Starsurfer IX and may be confiscated and disposed of if necessary."

Emma scoffed. "WAS IT NECESSARY, THOUGH? WHAT THE—"

The boys couldn't help but be worried seeing Emma like this.

The children were divided and split into three vehicles before they had any chance to use the book. Two robotic workers escorted each of them, and upon entering the vehicle, a video began to play on a large screen. To the children, it felt oddly reminiscent of the old commercials coming on TV late at night when they were back home. It explained the planet's infrastructure, its civilization, and the role each citizen, or rather "unit" according to the screen, played in society. A narrator, which sounded relatively human yet cryptic, began to speak while several diagrams were displayed on the screen. It explained that everyone on this planet was assigned a task to help maintain the planet's progress. In reality, for many, this commitment to progress was nothing more than a prison. None of the planet's inhabitants were allowed to simply "be." Instead, they had to work, and their labor would gradually earn them their right to "live." Naturally, the three friends would be no exception.

Separated from his friends, Shiloh was nervous but more determined than ever. He had his eyes on finding the table. Emma, too, was focused on figuring things out before they got worse, as she knew they would, having read the plot of *Starsurfers* a few times. Logan, however, was not appreciating being held captive. They struggled to force him into the vehicle, and while there, he was barely paying any attention to the video that played and spent most of the time screaming profanities at his captors. The three vehicles zoomed off, and the children had little to do but be forced to listen to this dystopian propaganda on their way to their destinations. Upon landing, Emma, Shiloh, and Logan were each given a task specific to them. Logan and Shiloh were allocated to an area separate from Emma. Meanwhile, Emma's vehicle had landed in a much more remote location, which looked like a facility of some sort.

The boys disembarked their vehicles, and Shiloh noticed Logan being escorted out by the robotic personnel.

"YOU WORMS FOR BRAINS!" shouted Logan.

Shiloh couldn't help but smile, hearing his friend's familiar yet deafening voice.

The boys were then led to an elevator that took them to a hotter area. This was where the space civilization attempted to build more habitable quarters inside the planet. These areas would be closer to the planet's core and made using a rare element called neutronium, also used to fabricate their vehicles. They had harvested this rare substance from the planet, once called "Starsurfers VIII," and collectivized it through their scientific methods. Sadly, this happened only months before their forces tried to gather as much neutronium as possible and quickly reached the planet's core, where they were forced to adapt and live, later renaming the world "Starsurfers IX."

Shiloh and Logan were brought closer to the core, and it felt much hotter. Before they exited the elevator, the personnel escorting them gave the boys suits to wear that would allow for their safe travel in the heat. Both suits were made of pure diamond, a detail Logan seemed to enjoy.

"You don't got to tell me twice," said Logan, glaring at the reflective jewels that encrusted the outside of his suit.

Shiloh put his on as well, though he thought it was a bit too big on him. He didn't know what was "too big" here anyway, so he didn't mention it. They were brought out onto a balcony a thousand kilometers above the core, which felt extremely close. There were frames of metal exposed to the open planet's center intended for the heatproof neutronium paneling that the boys would be working on.

"Woah," Shiloh muttered under his breath, looking over the edge of their workstation to see a hot, bright, yet beautiful ball of light. Something about it was different though. How could they be so close and still survive?

The civilization had somehow encased the planet's core in a membrane of some sort, different from how they'd created the outer protective shell. This membrane was almost frothy, and it was hard to tell what it was made from, but if Shiloh had to guess, it looked a lot like water.

"This way, human," commanded the robots in unison as they motioned the boys to a particular area of the workstation that held odd items they had never seen before.

"These are electromagnetic welding guns. These will be your tools to fuse the panels to the framework," explained the two robots. "Simply lay the panels down and use the tools to secure the corners."

They then handed each of the boys a handheld tool that looked unlike any technology they might've seen before. Shortly after, the robot personnel disappeared, leaving the boys to contemplate the intricacies of their newfound space gadgets.

"How do you think it works?" asked Shiloh, genuinely curious about this exciting piece of alien material.

"Not sure. Looks sort of like a blaster to me, you know, like from space movies?" replied Logan.

He walked over to a pile of panels stacked against the railing, picked one up, and set it down where they were supposed to add them. He then pressed the tool to the corner of the panel as it was aligned correctly on the frame. A quick yet alarmingly aggressive sounding hum of vibration was heard by the boys. A few seconds after contemplating what had just happened, they tried to shift the panel yet found there was an invisible bond between the panel's corner and the framework underneath.

"Well, I was close. It's more like a magnet gun. That's kind of cool, I guess," said Logan sarcastically.

The boys began to install the panels, as they figured they were probably being watched, but also used this time to talk.

"Shiloh, you probably know more than I do about this place since you've read the book, but what do you think happens when you die here?" asked Logan in a more serious and dulled tone than usual.

This question, oddly, hadn't crossed Shiloh's mind until now.

"I— I have no idea. I don't remember anybody dying in the book," replied Shiloh.

This thought wouldn't leave either of their minds for the next few moments as they continued laying down panel after panel and fusing them secure.

"Okay, look, you see that guard over there? Follow me and back me up. I think I have an idea," said Shiloh, to Logan's surprise.

They snuck a few yards over near the guard with the guise of discussing their plans for installing panels and other areas they could work on to achieve a faster result.

"Don't do anything stupid, dude. We still have to find Emma," Logan reminded Shiloh.

The boys sat behind a stack of panels. At the same time, they observed the guard checking the perimeter every few seconds and then moving to another post, where it would oversee another area. As the guard turned to make its way to the other post, Shiloh went into a full sprint and left Logan looking confused. In only a few seconds, Shiloh had run up behind the guard and pulled the trigger on his welding tool, which at this point, seemed a lot cooler to Logan because it exploded the alien's head dramatically.

Logan couldn't believe his eyes. His scrawny schoolmate had just taken out one of the guards holding them captive. Though, his awe was quickly replaced with fear again as two more guards appeared. One of them was swift to identify the threat and hit the tool out of Shiloh's hand; then they proceeded to close in on him.

One of the guards grabbed Shiloh by the ribs, and the other grabbed him by the neck. Logan couldn't tear his eyes away from the scene before realizing the time was now or never. He swiftly ran up to the two guards who were focused on eliminating Shiloh and, much like in an action movie, ran up the spine of one robot and, as he jumped off, shot it in its head. As he landed, he was met with surprise. The other robot had noticed and directed its focus onto Logan, and grabbed the gun from his hands as he landed. The robot now had it pointed directly at his face. Realizing this was probably the end, Logan shut his eyes, only to hear the sovereign sound of the welding tool. He was confused, however, as to how he could hear it without trouble. As the robot was about to terminate Logan, it was shot in the head by Shiloh using his welding tool, which he had picked up when the guards were focused on Logan.

"Bro… that was sick! Did you just see me?! And YOU! YOU'RE JUST A LITTLE BADASS NOW, AREN'T YOU?" yelled Logan excitedly. "But, but seriously, you saved my life, Shiloh! Thank you."

Shiloh looked down and smiled. "You saved mine too, bro. Sounds to me that we are both lucky."

This was the first time the boys had truly felt lucky to have the other present.

"You know what, I figure fear isn't a thing for these robo-douchebags, but I think without it, we wouldn't be alive," said Logan thoughtfully.

Shiloh nodded and pondered on that idea for a second before they decided they should keep moving.

"Now, let's go find Emma and get out of here. Hopefully, she's found the table by now," said Shiloh.

Logan nodded, and the boys ran off to find their friend, though they had no idea where the robots might have taken her.

Chapter 6
Hide Your Tears

When the children were separated, the boys ended up being brought to the same area. However, Emma wasn't as lucky. Her eyes opened to see nothing but pitch-darkness. Her uneven breath was the only sound she could make out. Trying her best not to panic, Emma slowed her breathing and focused on her thoughts instead, even if they, too, were racing at a thousand miles a second. She wondered where her friends were. And, more importantly, where was she? Emma recalled bits and pieces of the robots forcing her to separate from her friends but could remember nothing past being shoved in the vehicle. She reached out her arms but could not extend them very far or walk anywhere. She was confined to this planet's prison cells, like an ancient pharaoh to his sarcophagus.

After a moment more of panic, she collected herself. "Why does it have to smell like crayons?" muttered Emma, consumed with discomfort.

The inside of the cell showed no signs of an exit, and she had finally realized she was stuck. Emma didn't have any of her belongings because the robots had confiscated them. This meant she couldn't use the book and pencil to alter her circumstances as the boys had before.

"Shiloh… Logan… please hurry," whispered Emma, as she tried to conserve what oxygen she had in this container as best as she could.

With her eyes adjusting to the dark, she sat there waiting for her friends to turn up, but after about two hours in her cell, she began to see patterns emerge from the darkness. These patterns resembled the temporary blotch in vision one might have after looking at the sun, though she didn't feel any of the pain.

Emma found herself living an out-of-body experience as she focused on these ever-changing patterns.

What is happening? Emma thought to herself. She began to correlate the patterns she saw with points in time that were emotional for her. Tears rolled down her cheek; she was lost in such an intriguing world, despite currently being locked in a cell. The darkness was making her look deeper into herself than any mirror could. Meanwhile, the boys were on their way to find her.

Somehow, Shiloh and Logan had managed to steal one of the UFOs and were now landing it on a cliff not far from the planet's core.

After landing, the boys exited the automated vehicle, ran a few feet to an archway, and took cover behind a corner.

"Alright, follow me," said Logan as he brushed past Shiloh, running a few feet ahead.

"Wait!" said Shiloh, stopping Logan in his tracks. "We need to find Emma. Don't run off yet. We don't even know if she's in there!"

"What in the hell do you think I'm trying to do, you idiot?"

"*You're* trying to do?" Shiloh snapped. "We're both trying to save her! Why does everything always have to be about you? *Oh, I'm hungry. I can't go on because I don't have a Snickers bar to keep me from being a complete asshat.*"

Logan looked at Shiloh, confused. It was odd to hear him use curse words when he was usually so reserved. The back-and-forth bickering made both of the boys snap.

"You wonder why people pick on you, Shiloh. It's HILARIOUS! You're so insecure about yourself that you can't even tell her you like her, and you're worried that I'm going to save her before you do and seem like the knight in shining armor."

Shiloh scoffed and shook his head, his eyes meeting the foreign dirt beneath him in embarrassment.

"Yeah, you are," said Logan, laughing.

Shiloh's face was now red with anger. "I don't like her!"

Logan smiled. "Good. Because GUESS WHAT? I DO!"

Hearing this from Logan made Shiloh's heart sink deep into his stomach. He didn't want to hear that Logan had feelings for Emma because he didn't think he had a chance with her if Logan was his competition. He was sure Emma would rather have a more robust, more secure partner like Logan than a scrawny, unmotivated loser like himself.

"But… but… you can't like her. I… I love her," Shiloh replied, defeated.

To Shiloh's surprise, Logan started laughing. "You love her," said Logan. "HAHA! You literally have zero chances with a babe like that, dude."

This type of heated competition was something Logan was used to, but Shiloh, on the other hand, had never really been the determined type. However, there was also pride somewhere amid the embarrassment of admitting his feelings to Logan. He knew how he felt about Emma and was not going to focus on the fact that Logan liked her, too. He knew what he had to do.

"Look," said Shiloh, clearing his through and wiping the tears from his eyes, "I know I play the victim more than anybody should. I know that. But Emma… she's in trouble, so we can't afford the luxury of fighting about this, okay? If you like her, that's fine. Let's just save her before it's too late."

This made Logan choke up and forget his anger, realizing that Shiloh was right.

"I'm… I'm sorry, Shiloh," said Logan apologetically. "I've been a real dick. It hasn't been fair to you. I know that. There's just always been something about you that ticked me off."

Logan was shedding a few tears, but it seemed like he was holding back more than he was letting out. "Honestly, man, I'm just… I could never… be as smart as you or as interested in ANYTHING as you. Everything just seems so hopeless that I don't wish for much anymore. You always have your head in a book or are off doing something that makes you happy. Then there's me, always being a dick, but then I worry about what people think, and I just feel so lost. I didn't think I would become so mean just trying to be somebody that wasn't what I thought of as weak."

Until now, Logan had never looked at himself from any perspective but his own. Like Emma contemplating in the darkness, Logan and Shiloh both had to take a deeper look at who they were and who they wanted to be.

Shiloh walked up to Logan, whose eyes were full of tears now. "Hey, hide your tears. You don't want Emma to think I beat you up or something."

This made Logan chuckle as his friend wiped the tears off his cheek.

The boys noticed where they were, and both realized how lucky they were not to be seen by any of the swarming guards. They waited for their moment to run past some guards in a courtyard that surrounded an enormous building. The boys were moving from shadow to shadow, not even needing to use the welding tools they had picked up before. The giant building outside intrigued them, as it had tons of vehicles flying overhead and lots of robots guarding the surrounding area. Logan looked around to determine their next move, while Shiloh focused on the vehicles overhead.

"Look, dude," whispered Shiloh, "the ships are landing on the building and disappearing."

Logan looked and also thought it peculiar.

"You think she's in there?" asked Shiloh.

"Maybe there is a way inside from up there," said Logan, motivated to save his friend and get out of this book.

The boys ran back in the vehicle's direction they had used to land there, and Shiloh followed close behind. They programmed the vehicle to fly them high above the building to get a better view.

"That's got to be it," the boys said in unison.

After that, they immediately set the vehicle to descend into the hollow, heavily guarded building.

"I sure hope Emma's in there. Otherwise, we're—" said Logan.

"Toast."

Chapter 7

The Pit of Souls

Emma coughed as she was having difficulty breathing inside the damp, coffin-shaped cell. She was drifting in and out of consciousness, and each time she would wake up, she would panic for a few seconds until remembering how she had gotten there. She constantly wondered where the boys were, and her mind would, at times, take more bleak paths, imagining the worst possible scenarios. Her bag, having been confiscated by the robots, was of no use to her or the boys. The table was nowhere to be found, either.

Everything seemed hopeless as the hours in the cell felt like days. Meanwhile, the outside of her cell was just as quiet as the inside. Other human-like figures were being escorted by the robots into cells to be imprisoned for whatever reason. Unlike Emma and the boys, the prisoners, too, also benefitted from technological enhancements, giving them a cyborg-like appearance. Yet, even so, they still seemed much more "human" than the robot authority currently suffocating the planet.

* * *

The boys were descending quickly toward the landing pad atop the building that held Emma captive. Time felt surreal in this place, almost like it didn't exist. It was all just constant motion and labor that never seemed to cease. The boys looked around at the bleak, soul-ridden dystopia as they floated down.

"Do you think she's in there?" asked Shiloh.

"She better be," replied Logan with a grim look on his face. "Otherwise, I'm using this thing to kill as many of those terminator-wannabes as I can in there."

Shiloh looked over at his friend, unsure of how to feel but determined not to fail in their quest.

Their vehicle made contact with the landing pad as expected, shortly after being followed by the elevator mechanism lowering them and their ship further down into the building.

"Woah!" the boys exclaimed in unison.

They couldn't believe their eyes. Tiny cells aligned the halls of every level, and guards were assigned to keep watch, with lines of prisoners being escorted in and out.

"She's got to be in here," said Shiloh.

"Look. The second those doors open, Shiloh, they're going to try to turn US into ONE OF THOSE," said Logan, pointing from himself to the prisoner cells. "We must stick together. Otherwise, we lose our shot at finding Emma and getting back home."

Shiloh nodded. Their descent had finally halted, and the boys held their breath until the UFO's doors opened. They expected to be greeted by guards intending to capture them, but for now, no one seemed to have noticed that the boys were there.

Shiloh and Logan scoured the area, drowned by the commotion around them. They checked every cell in a bid to find their friend, careful not to attract any unwanted attention from the robot guards.

"Not her, not her, not her," Logan and Shiloh muttered as they dashed past hundreds of translucent, cocoon-looking cells.

"EMMA! EMMA! ARE YOU THERE?"

Unluckily for the boys, a prisoner on a floor below had caught sight of them and pointed them out, alerting the guards who were now in pursuit. With their window of time to escape running short, the boys were losing hope that they'd ever find their friend.

"There's got to be over a hundred thousand cells in here," said Shiloh.

Now worried about their lack of progress, Logan screamed at the top of his lungs, "EMMA, IF YOU CAN HEAR US, SPIN IN CIRCLES!"

Shiloh realized the genius of what Logan had just said, being that each prisoner was forced to stand in their cell.

The plan worked, and Emma began to spin. Her movement quickly stood out to Logan and Shiloh as they scouted the remaining floors.

"There she is!" exclaimed Shiloh.

As they were about to make their way over to her, they stopped. The sudden shrieking of an alarm pierced their ears and made them fall to their knees. The noise seemed to do nothing to the robot guards but brought severe pain to everyone else in the building. The boys noticed that a group of robots was now running up the stairs toward them. Though the pain was almost unbearable, Shiloh stood up, grabbed Logan by the arm, and pulled him up.

"We have to save Emma!" he mouthed to Logan, unable to speak any louder with the loud frequency carving at their eardrums.

The boys ran up more flights of stairs. By the time the boys reached Emma's level, the robots chasing them had doubled in numbers. They were climbing floors using a clever method of stacking on top of one another until they reached the same level the boys were on.

By a stroke of luck, Shiloh and Logan made it to Emma's cell in time, ripped open the flesh-like door, and freed her. However, the perfect silence that she had experienced as a prisoner quickly transformed into a harrowing feeling of dread, making the girl pass out seconds after being freed.

In a bid to buy them more time, Shiloh was using his makeshift weapon to disable the guards one by one, and to his surprise, he wasn't half-bad at it. Logan, on the other hand, was on his knees, shaking Emma, but she wasn't responding. The boy then picked her up and threw her over his shoulder.

"Time to LEAVE!" he shouted.

Shiloh was surprised that Logan was strong enough to hold her up. They both used their weapons to disable the horde of guards swarming around them. One by one, the boys eliminated the robots and went down flight by flight, only to be greeted by more. Logan was impressed with Shiloh, as he had never seen the boy stand up for himself. Eventually, they reached the ground level of the building where their ship was still waiting for them. They ran inside and quickly hit the button to close the doors.

Shiloh suddenly remembered that he needed to activate the elevator. Still, as he reopened the door to go out and do so, he noticed that a group of guards had already reached the control panel. The guards wouldn't let them get away that easily, but Shiloh had another plan.

In the meantime, Logan was caring for Emma, and she eventually woke up to see him. Emma smiled, then coughed a bit.

"Thank you, Logan," she said in a tired voice as she leaned in and kissed him on the cheek.

Shiloh had just closed the doors and turned around to see Emma plant a kiss on Logan's cheek. The boy felt overwhelmed by hopelessness again but realized they still had to get off the planet somehow.

"My backpack! It has all the books..." said Emma.

"Logan, you get on the wheel," interjected Shiloh.

Logan looked confused and replied, "There's a wheel?"

Shiloh leaned on the wall behind him and elbowed it. A loose panel flipped open, revealing a wheel, a gear stick, and a floor pedal that folded out from the wall. Logan was in disbelief, but quickly hopped on the wheel and pressed the big green button on the side of the revolution that he figured might mean "TAKEOFF."

As the vehicle was taking off, Logan pressed a tiny blue button on the gear stick knob, which made the entire vehicle transparent, allowing him to see all around him and navigate more safely.

Logan shifted gears and put his foot on the pedal. The robots had clicked a button that began closing the hole at the top of the building elevator that would be their escape. Yet they still had to find the books the robots had confiscated shortly after their arrival on the planet.

"Where did you guys get guns?" Emma asked, puzzled.

The boys grinned for a second.

"Borrowed them…" said Logan.

"From a friend," continued Shiloh.

They flew high across the buildings, looking around for a sign, when they noticed a small group of guards holding Emma's bag over the open panels above the planet's blinding core. It didn't take the children long to figure out that the guards would soon drop the books into the pit, and they would be stuck there without a way out. Upon seeing the guards let go of the bag, Logan relinquished his control of the vehicle.

"NOOO!" shouted Emma.

Shiloh stomped on the pedal and blasted forward at high speed, seizing the only chance they had. They sped closer and closer toward the core as the bag fell, and it was getting hotter.

"EMMA, OPEN THE DOOR AND CATCH IT ON THREE!" yelled Shiloh.

Emma and Logan thought the plan was crazy, but she quickly stood up and ran over to the door, stumbling as the vehicle shook.

"ONE, TWO… THREE!" yelled Shiloh, whipping the vehicle onto its side, allowing the now-open door to face upward. Emma clicked the door's opening mechanism but fell to the other side of the vehicle as Shiloh rolled it. Luckily, she caught the bag as it fell on her.

"SHILOH, YOU DID IT!" exclaimed Emma!

Yet, the children's excitement was short-lived because the vehicle's propulsion stopped working, and, just like that, they lost all power.

"Wait, what's happening?" asked Logan, trembling.

The vehicles speed and violent shaking progressed as it plunged straight into the scorching core of the planet. None of them knew what was going to happen next. After all, none of them knew what would happen if somebody died in the book. Soon after, unbearable heat overtook their senses, and their vision clouded.

Chapter 8

Know Thyself

Everything the children ever knew was now a distant memory. As the children were slowly coming to their senses, they again started wondering who and where they were. They were examining their clothes, not even remembering having put them on the day before. Hunger, pain, sadness, none of those things existed here. Time was also obsolete. As the minutes ticked on, the children continued to look around this confusing space. They couldn't see anything. Or rather anything besides the color white, themselves, and the colors of their clothes. The room they were in was an infinite white plane of nothing, stretching limitlessly into the horizon. A bag sat on the floor between them, its contents unknown.

Emma looked around the room and noticed the bag and the other two boys.

"Excuse me, where are we? And I'm sorry if I sound crazy, but WHO are we exactly?"

This question puzzled the boys as they, too, pondered on their odd circumstances. Having seen the bag, Logan crawled over to it and poured the contents onto the floor. These knick-knacks added many colors to the room, and this made the children feel good. They were books, and many looked oddly familiar once they took a closer look.

Shiloh was staring at the book covers and reading their titles, feeling like he had seen these publications before but unsure where. Emma was inspecting the books, too. She noticed the one she was holding had the name "C. J. Wingate" on the spine. She was completely unaware that the author's last name was her own, though she assumed these books might be hers because of the nostalgia she was feeling. Logan looked through the books just as clueless as before.

"I… I don't know who I am, either. I know I'm me, but I'm at a loss for words. Have we always been here?" asked Logan.

The other two didn't know what to answer.

"I'm not exactly sure, but if I had to guess, I'd say these books have something to do with it," Emma replied.

The children examined the books more closely.

"It seems the same author writes all these books. 'Wingate' is on all the spines," exclaimed Emma, thrilled she had found a clue.

Logan picked up a rather tattered book from the pile that didn't seem as vibrantly illustrated and immediately noticed that the spine didn't have a name on it. He started flicking through the dusty pages. Someone had written all over the inside of the cover with green ink. The added stimuli of color in this white expanse were even more of a reason to investigate their circumstances. Among the scribblings on the book cover, Logan spotted a name: "Seven Evans."

"Not this one," said Logan. "This one is nothing like those books. I don't think it's the same author at all. The only name I see mentioned here is 'Seven Evans.'"

The name rang a bell in Shiloh's mind. He remembered his grandfather's face and that it was Everett's nickname they had found in the book. With all these memories flooding his mind, the boy was able to remember his name.

"Shiloh," he said out loud. "We have the books, but wasn't there a table or something that was, like, the key to going places?" Emma asked.

The children all remembered the table at the mention of it. Then they heard a thick, noticeable "knock" echoing in their direction from a few feet behind them. They turned around, and there it was. Emma and Logan ran over to inspect it. Meanwhile, Shiloh was interested in looking through the book Logan had found in the pile. He ran his fingers over the words, feeling closer to his grandfather than he had been in a long time. His memory was finally back—for the most part, at least—and with it came the bittersweet feeling of missing his grandfather.

The book Shiloh held in his hands contained a lighthearted story about a family living together in a suburb. It seemed like an easy-to-follow yet insignificant story to follow at first. Shiloh was blazing through it quickly, yet as the plot became more sentimental, he slowed down his pace. The family in the story was affectionate, spending holidays playing games and sharing laughter over meals while enjoying each other's company. Reading this made Shiloh smile, so he continued. The grandfather in the family was a magician. He had a son whom he loved very much and a daughter-in-law who was one of the most beautiful women he had ever seen. The magician's son and daughter-in-law were married and had birthed and cared for a beautiful baby boy named Shiloh. Reading this passage gave Shiloh chills. He knew that the people his grandfather had written about were his parents, who had died in a train accident when Shiloh was just a baby, leaving his grandparents in charge of raising him.

Shiloh stopped reading, closed the little book, and walked over to his friends, who were still investigating the magic table.

"Shiloh, have you seen this thing?" asked Logan.

"Um, duh, dude," Shiloh replied. "How do you think we got here?"

Logan slowly recalled bits and pieces of when they were in *Starsurfers*.

"Wait a second," said Logan. "Are we… DEAD?!"

"We can't be dead," replied Emma. "I see you here right now, and I know YOU are actually YOU because I know my brain definitely wouldn't have dressed you like that. No offense."

Emma's humor made Shiloh laugh, lightening the mood for a short while.

Logan chuckled and replied, "WELL, JEEZ. THANKS, EMMA!"

The children were enjoying themselves for the first time in what seemed like days. After having been through so much, staying in this simplified plane of existence, where all they had was each other, was a welcome change.

Shiloh remembered the book he had just browsed through and knew he had to tell his friends about it.

"Guys, I have to tell you something," said Shiloh. "This book… You're right, Logan. It doesn't fit in with the other ones we found in the backpack earlier."

Logan and Emma read deeper into the first few pages of the dusty book, but they still didn't get it. Thankfully, Shiloh was there to help fill in any gaps. He wasn't completely sure, but he had a feeling that this book held the answer to finding his grandfather.

"Wait, so your grandpa wrote a story about a WHOLE other family and decided to live there instead of with YOU, in REALITY?" asked Logan. "Wouldn't that make you want to, like… you know… not want to find him?"

"That family that he wrote about was, well…" Shiloh fell silent.

Emma could see tears welling up in Shiloh's eyes, taking her back to the art class they were in together just a few days ago.

"Those were your parents that he wrote about. Shiloh, I— I can't imagine how you're feeling right now," said Emma.

"That's what I wanted to talk to you guys about," said Shiloh. He cleared his throat and continued, "So we've been through a lot. And I… I've been dragging you both through all these books, risking EVERYTHING including our lives… just to find my grandpa. Before we left, it seemed like it really wouldn't be that hard, but after all that we've been through with this"—Shiloh paused in appreciation—"this incredible table, I can't ask you two to keep risking your lives for me."

The other two understood what he meant. After all, they had been through more mind-shattering events in their short time together than they had in their entire lives. Yet, Emma wasn't quite ready to give up, and neither was Logan.

"Shiloh, what if your grandpa wrote this to be with your parents again because he missed them?" said Emma.

The thought had already crossed Shiloh's mind. "Then, I'm going in alone. I'm extremely thankful for everything you two have gone through for me, and I don't want to put you through any more trouble than I already have."

These words pushed a button for Logan, and though he understood where Shiloh was coming from, he had to speak up. "Bro, you are right. We have been through a LOT, and I've only remembered bits and pieces of it so far, but I wouldn't say it's all for you. My dad made this thing with his bare hands, and your grandpa added magic to it, dude… literal magic."

Logan's kindness made Shiloh smile as he wiped his wet, stuffy nose.

Logan continued, "And Emma, your mom created entire realities just by writing them down, and we could experience them in… the scariest but most KICKASS way! Remember our science teacher, Mrs. Ravencroft? She would crap herself if she saw any of this. The whole world would, I bet!"

Shiloh could see where Logan was going with this.

"I know you feel you're alone in this," said Logan, "but if you think about it, each of us is here for a reason, dude. MY dad made this thing, and YOUR grandpa used magic to make it into… well, THIS! And Emma, your mom wrote books that created these worlds! I totally would've left by now in all this craziness. Well, maybe the old me would have, but now I couldn't see myself leaving my best friends behind when we're literally THIS close to getting what we came for. So, I'm with you, dude."

Emma was touched, as she had never seen this tender side to Logan before.

"WE are with you…." Chimed in Emma. "Until the end."

Shiloh wiped the tears from his broad smile and opened his arms to his friends, who came in to embrace him.

"Are you sure?" Shiloh asked again, squeezed by his two best friends. The other two just hugged him even harder. Shiloh closed his eyes, dropped the little book from his hands onto the table, and muttered the same words that had taken them on the most life-changing journey they'd ever been on: *"Quod est superius est sicut quod inferius."*

As the table's runes began to glow, Shiloh placed his hand on the surface and clutched tight onto his friends. Soon after, the table's low humming frequency rose in pitch until it became unintelligible. WHOOSH! With that, the children were gone, off to hopefully find Shiloh's grandfather once and for all.

Chapter 9

You Look Like You've Just Seen a Ghost!

Before they had even opened their eyes, the children noticed the smell of their environment completely change from cool, thin air to a warm, fragrant one. It was oddly nostalgic for Shiloh, but he couldn't figure out why. The children all felt an odd sensation of something touching them on their backs and shoulders, so they opened their eyes to see what it was. It was clothes.

They were standing in a closet with only a few winter coats, but the thick fabric of them was enough to crowd the small space.

"Ouch, you stepped on my foot!" whispered Emma.

The children were shuffling around, trying to stay quiet while also figuring out their surroundings.

"Sorry," said Shiloh, "it's not my fault the table shoved us in this closet like some sardines in a can."

The children did their best to compose themselves and started discussing what they should do next.

"You should go first, you know," said Logan. "Since it's your family? We'll wait here until you need us or something."

Emma nodded. "Makes sense."

A chill ran down Shiloh's spine. He was suddenly nervous, thinking of all the possible outcomes, the things he would say, and whether any of this even mattered. He gulped so loud that his friends both put their hands on his shoulders to motivate him.

"You got this, bro," said Logan.

Emma gave Shiloh a wink, which also helped a bit.

Shiloh opened the closet door and shut it behind him.

"Hey, you finally came out of the closet!" whispered Logan.

Shiloh smiled and took a deep breath, then looked around at the room he was in. It was a bedroom—his bedroom, except it looked different. The smell that filled the air was of pine and vanilla. He noticed the window had been left open, and outside, only a few dozen feet away, was a giant pine forest, the very same one he had grown up with. He was home. Or rather as close to home as the pages of the book would allow. He tried not to forget this.

Shiloh noticed a candle, and assumed it was the source of the vanilla scent he was experiencing, but he didn't care to check to see if he was right. Looking around him, Shiloh noticed the walls were painted in cream colors, differently from how his room back home really was, which was white. A king-sized bed sat in the middle of the room, dressed in dark-gray sheets and big, fluffy pillows with an olive-green comforter that reminded him of the one in his own room. He wondered if it was the same. On each side of the bed were black wooden dressers and one side was decorated with a jewelry box and a box of tissues, while the other dresser had an ashtray and a copy of C. J. Wingate's *Starsurfers* with a pair of reading glasses atop.

"This must've been mom and dad's room," said Shiloh under his breath. The hairs on his arms began to stand up, followed by goosebumps.

As he approached the door that led into the hallway, a pair of voices that didn't seem to sound like his two friends grew louder. Shiloh stealthily cracked open the door and peered through with one eye, trying to spot the source of the noise that seemed to be coming from what should be the dining room down the hallway. He took a deep breath and walked out of the bedroom.

So many thoughts were racing through Shiloh's head, but he reminded himself that none of this was "real" to help cope with his electrifying anxiety.

One memory, in particular, was of when he was only four years old. His grandfather Everett was reading him a bedtime story while his parents were on vacation. The TV began to make noise from another room, so his grandfather went to grab it, and a few minutes later, he returned to finish Shiloh's bedtime story. The tone, however, was much different from before. He was also reading much slower, as if Everett wasn't focused on the story he was telling. In retrospect, Shiloh realized this was the first time he saw his life change after losing his parents. It felt odd to be now walking towards what sounded like them.

The boy entered the open area of the house and, to his surprise, saw three familiar faces: Two of them were glowing with joy as they stared back at him, while the other seemed happy and distraught in equal measure.

"Hey, son," said Shiloh's father.

"We were just talking about you, dear! How was your day at school?" asked his mother.

Seeing his parents again was already bringing an infectious smile to his face, yet his mother's words threw him off. Shiloh's grandfather was smiling as he watched him reunite with his parents, yet he seemed a bit tired and less enthusiastic about his grandson's visit. Everett greeted the boy with a nod of his bald, wrinkly head.

"Mom, Dad, I thought you two were…." Shiloh said with a lump in his throat.

Everett quickly replied, "Gone? No, they're back from their vacation, Shiloh! All is well."

Everett then turned to face the two young parents. "He's missed you both! We all have, but we're glad to have you back home."

Shiloh didn't like the direction this conversation was heading, as it looked like his grandfather was reluctant to admit that this reality wasn't real. He knew something was off, and felt that his parents, most likely, had no idea that they, too, were not real. They both stared at Shiloh with love in their eyes.

"What's wrong, sweetie?" his mother asked. "You look like you've just seen a ghost!"

Shiloh fell silent, not knowing what to say. One thing that was clear was that he didn't realize how much he had missed them. It was all flooding back as he sat there, and he found himself wanting more and more of this blissful moment.

Shiloh walked to his dad and sat on his knee. His father gave him a warm hug, and Shiloh felt so welcomed in his arms. All the love that was robbed from him growing up was now overwhelming him with a sense of safety, yet he didn't know if he should trust the feeling.

Meanwhile, Everett, whom the children were here to save, acted suspicious and different from what Shiloh had expected. He thought his grandfather would be stuck somewhere waiting for him to come and save him, but it seemed that he was staying there of his own free will.

Everett missed his family that was so tragically taken from him, so he used his magic one last time to create a world where they still existed. Having used the table for all of his other quests in pursuit of the world's most ancient mysteries, Everett grew tired. One night, after pondering on the death of his beloved son and daughter-in-law, Everett decided he would be finished with the table for good after one last adventure. He would write a short, sweet novella about his lost loved ones and the happy life they lived that, along with the table's power, would allow them to live on in this bubble reality he had created. The best part was that he could stay with them endlessly. However, Everett couldn't write his wife or grandson into the story. After all that he had learned throughout his travels, people who were still alive could not be brought to life inside another reality or dimension because they were tied to their own. Only after somebody died could their soul wander and be fractally linked to another reality.

For Everett, giving up everything he had in exchange for his son's return was a great sacrifice. Still, in the end, he inevitably decided it was a worthy decision.

While Shiloh was still trying to make sense of this strange family reunion, his friends grew tired of waiting in the closet. Emma and Logan snuck out of the room, eager to see what was going on. They hid behind a hallway corner, watching the four of them interact. Logan, standing behind Emma, was briefly distracted by the smell of her hair. He thought it baffling that her hair could smell as lovely as it did after everything they had been through. As Logan was mid-thought, Emma turned around and stared at him with a puzzled face. She shook her head and returned her gaze to the family.

Shiloh enjoyed having his parents back but was confused, thankful, and sad, all at the same time.

"Mom, Dad, how old am I?" he asked, unsure what to expect.

Everett heard this and glared at the boy, but Shiloh paid him no mind. He was determined to free himself and his parents from this illusion.

"Well, how silly of a question is that," his mother replied with a smile. "Your father and I haven't forgotten about you, if that's what you're thinking! My little boy, you're getting big now, aren't you? I suppose you're the same as I was, finishing first grade, the youngest of your class, only four years old. How I relish these moments watching you grow up. I'm so proud of you, son."

Shiloh's heart felt heavier than when his grandfather told him his parents wouldn't be "coming back" when he was still a toddler. In reality, the boy looked three times as old as the four-year-old toddler his mother was seeing.

"You're much taller than I was at your age," his father added. "When I was a little tike like yourself, I wasn't, well… so 'little.' Ain't that right, pops?"

He looked over at Everett, who was sitting with his head resting in his palm, staring off into the distance.

Everett seemed lost in thought. He often saw that dreadful day of his son's death while staring in his son's eyes, and though they were face to face, it felt bittersweet each moment spent here, knowing the unforgettable truth. Shortly after processing his son's question, he sprang to life again and answered, "Why, that's right! You were a chubby little one. Could never keep your hand out of the cookie jar, could you?"

Shiloh smiled, yet tears rolled down his cheek. His grandfather saw this and let out a heavy sigh of exhaustion. Shiloh hopped off of his father's lap and walked over to face his grandfather.

"Grandpa," sobbed Shiloh, "I came here to save you, to bring you back home to your real life, the one that you left behind, to the people you left behind. I've felt lost for as long as I can remember, but I guess that's what happens when you lose people you love more than a few times. I just never thought that it would be like THIS."

Everett rubbed his chin, not knowing how to respond at first. He thought of his wife, Faith, and memories of the previous life he had chosen to leave behind. One by one, they came flooding back, and Everett's eyes filled with tears.

"You're right, Shiloh," said Everett. "You look just like your father."

Everett squeezed Shiloh tight, grateful that the boy had risked his life just to come and save him from an illusion where he would constantly be reminded of the death of his son. He realized how selfish his actions must have looked to the family he'd left behind.

Logan and Emma, on the other hand, were quietly discussing when exactly the right time would be to step out and make an appearance, if there ever was one. Logan almost stepped out when he saw Everett begin to tear up. Emma grabbed him by the collar of his shirt, holding him back.

"We can't mess this up. We only have one chance at getting this right and return home!" she said.

Shiloh's mom and dad were looking at Shiloh and his grandfather, looking confused but happy, as if their emotions could vary little from a state of everlasting contentment.

"Hey, dad," said Shiloh's father to Everett, "show Shiloh some of your card tricks, will you?

Clara and I are going to walk down the road to the corner store and grab some Cokes. Do y'all want one?"

Everett squeezed Shiloh a bit harder and waved goodbye as he replied, "Sounds good, son."

The young couple smiled, grabbed their coats, and walked out, leaving their family, but in an entirely different manner this time. Shiloh and his grandfather knew it would be the last time they would see them. After the front door had shut, Shiloh collapsed into his grandfather's arms, and Everett began to sob as well, embracing his grandson, whom he had missed dearly.

"I promise not to disappear again, Shiloh," said Everett. "I'm sorry I left you and your grandmother behind. I suppose you're old enough now to realize that what I did was wrong. You've gotten taller, too! You must be… ten years old now?"

Shiloh chuckled. "I'm twelve, Grandpa."

Having watched everything unfold from afar, Logan and Emma believed it was now the right time to reveal themselves.

"He sure acts like a ten-year-old, though," said Logan playfully across the hall.

Shiloh heard this voice and realized he had forgotten his friends were waiting for him and felt guilty about it.

"You're one to talk," replied Emma, also stepping out from behind the corner.

Shiloh looked at his friends, waved at them to come over, then looked up at his grandfather.

"Grandpa, these are my friends," said Shiloh.

"No, Shiloh," said Everett. "These are your best friends. Nothing short of a best friend would have your back in a place like this."

Everett's comment lingered for a bit, making them think. The children stared at each other, realizing just how right Shiloh's grandfather was, and they accepted it.

Chapter 10
Imagine, Anywhere

"Hello, sir," said Emma, introducing herself to Everett, who was thrilled to meet Shiloh's friends.

"I'm Logan," said Logan abruptly as he waved toward Everett, who waved back, then walked over to talk to Emma.

Though Everett was a skilled magician and undoubtedly had a lot of power, this was not normally what people would see upon first meeting him. He came off as a sweet, old man that had been through more ups and downs than most people. Though wielding magic for so many years had weathered his mind a bit, Everett cared for his family, and it showed when he spoke because his eyes communicated how he felt just as plainly as his words.

Everett looked down at the girl below who was much shorter than him.

"You must be Miss Emma Wingate, of course," said Everett.

Emma was happy to know that he remembered her name. The two of them had met years earlier at the yard sale, where Emma's mother bought the table. It was then that Everett had noticed little

Emma and laughed at how interested she was in almost everything there.

"Here are your books, sir," stuttered Emma.

She handed him her backpack, which was full of her mother's books.

"Thank you, sweetheart. We can add them to the shelves later," said Everett, proud to be friends with the daughter of one of his favorite authors.

They talked for a bit about Everett's appreciation for her mother's books, and Emma was flattered. Over the past few days, she had come to truly discover the beauty that was her mother's writing. Their relationship had always felt distant due to a lack of understanding. From Emma's perspective, her mother never had enough time for her, but there was always plenty of time for writing. Though, now she understood that her mother was part of something bigger, and so was she.

Emma and Everett finished talking and turned to face the boys sitting in the living room. A big, teary-eyed smile crept on Emma's face at the sight of the two. Logan, who was lying on the couch, kicked his feet up and started snoring. Meanwhile, Shiloh was feeling odd about the unsettling feeling of being home and sad knowing that he'd be leaving his parents, or at least the living memory of them, behind.

"So, if we're all done lallygagging," said Emma, "I think I have a few places I'd like to visit before we head back home."

"Oh, I like her!" said Everett. "What did you have in mind?"

Shiloh got up from his seat to brainstorm with Emma and his grandfather. Logan, who heard them talking, got up quickly, eager to join the conversation.

"Wait, wait, wait," said Logan. "We should pick a book that we ALL want to go into. I'm not going into some girly romance novel."

Emma looked at Logan with an exhausted look on her face. "Oh, all right. Any ideas, then?"

Shiloh replied, "While I'm totally down to keep exploring, too, I think heading back home first might be best. We can shower, eat, you know… just regroup ourselves first, right? I want to ditch this feeling of being in purgatory."

The children agreed it was time to go, but Everett wanted to share something before leaving. He told them to follow him down the hall to his study. In this fictitious reality, this same room that the children had started their journey in was just as real, if not more colorful and better decorated than the real thing. As they entered the study, the table was waiting for them. It didn't seem to have a single scratch on it or any sign of damage that would indicate it had been used to travel between dimensions.

The room smelled of patchouli and tobacco, and there were more books on the shelves than Everett had in his original study back in the real world. The room was enchanting to the children, and they spent a moment just observing all the intricate items around them. The most impressive part of the room, of course, was the bookshelves. They were not arranged by their authors' last names, by date, or even by genre. They were organized by color.

"You see, Shiloh, before I set out to plant myself here with your mom and dad, I thought of all the things I could bring from the real world to keep me company. I couldn't bring you and your grandmother, of course. Or so I thought," said Everett, who began to lose his train of thought. "Anyway, I brought all my books. Some of these I used to read to you when you were younger. I can't think of a better place to find a book to explore!"

Logan coughed and mumbled under his breath, "Ever heard of a library?"

Everett smirked at the boy's sarcastic remark but continued, "I've gone quite deeply into about, oh, three or four hundred or so of the couple thousand books here, but I can tell you there isn't a book here you won't want to visit. I threw out all of my old books because I wanted to start fresh. Every book that I added to my collection since has seemed worthy of exploration. Though, I agree that preparations might be made to ensure we are well energized for the expedition! Home sounds like a good start. I've got some people to see."

Everett seemed eager to explore his collection further now that he had others to do it with. After all, the children were the first "real" people to see it and the table.

The children spent a few minutes looking through the wall of books that were arranged so neatly that they were afraid to remove them from their spots.

"Don't be afraid. Grab one. They don't bite," said Everett, his voice echoing through the large room.

"Yeah, until you go into a book with a mean ol' dog in it. THEN it bites!" mumbled Logan, earning him a chuckle from his companions.

This was the best moment the children thought they had had on their entire trip.

Logan had climbed a ladder that allowed easier access to the bookshelves and slid from one side of the room to the other. It was nearly ten feet tall and about half of the room's height. Another ladder would allow readers to access the other ten feet of shelves and books, which ranged from colors blue to purple. Still, it did not connect to the ground, and it could only be used by climbing the bottom ladder, which was extremely tedious.

When Shiloh asked about the upper level of blue and purple books, all his grandfather had to say was that if the children could reach them, they would be able to read them. Unfortunately, Everett's back wouldn't allow him to be of much help and access the upper levels as he used to in the past. After about an hour of exploring the study, the children finally decided which books they wanted to select for their future explorations. Every book on every shelf was so different from the books next to them, and that was Everett's favorite thing about his study. Every time he wanted to read or explore something new, it would happen.

Logan was looking at a series of adventure books titled *Witches and Wizards of Ancient Times* in the yellow and green area of the bookshelves and settled on the first volume in the series. Emma browsed around the red and orange area of the bookshelves and found herself hooked to a romance novella titled *The Way Back Home*, which she found to also be highly relevant. The story also seemed to feature an ongoing battle between aliens, werewolves, and vampires that had her intrigued, and though it seemed a risky dive, she didn't think twice about grabbing it.

In the end, Shiloh didn't end up with a book of his own because he felt that any book his friends had picked was worth exploring. After all, they had followed him through quite a few stories already. It was now his turn to let his friends decide on their next adventure.

Everett stood there, watching them, holding his old, little booklet close to his heart. He looked at Shiloh, who was leaning on the bookshelf, watching his friends scour the study.

"Hey, kiddo. I want to tell you something," said Everett.

Shiloh turned and faced his grandfather.

"I love you," said Everett, choking up. "And I'm sorry… that everything had to be this way. I love… I loved your mom and dad, Shiloh."

Shiloh also began to tear up listening to his grandfather because he could feel that the old man meant it.

"I know this place isn't real, but… they were real enough for me."

"Grandpa, I didn't know how to feel when I first got here. At first, I was mad. I couldn't imagine how you could do something… that felt so unreal."

Everett hung his head in shame.

"Yet after a while of being here, though, and talking to them, I started to see why you did it. I didn't realize how much I missed them, too. They're addicting to listen to."

Everett's face cracked into a smile, realizing his grandson could relate to how he was feeling.

"I forgive you, Grandpa. I probably would've done the same thing," said Shiloh.

This made Everett feel less alone in his actions and was exactly what he needed to hear in order to be able to move on from this fictitious reality.

Logan and Emma were now also listening in on the conversation.

"The truth is, though," Everett continued, "I'm afraid I don't know how I'm going even to BEGIN telling your grandmother about everything."

"Tell her the truth, Grandpa," replied Shiloh. "She'll understand."

Everett smiled. He knew his grandson was right. He thought him wise for his age, which also reminded him of his son. He was excited to watch his grandson's life unfold.

"I'm coming with you, you little rascals. Every story needs a grandpa! Before we leave, though, I say we go back home, our REAL home, for the night. I want to see Faith again, tell her about my adventures, and that I'm back for good."

"She won't be happy to hear that you're leaving so soon again," said Shiloh. "She's waited so long to see you! I don't know if she can stand to be apart while we go off on adventures and have fun."

Everett nodded and replied, "Well, then, maybe we'll have to take her with us, won't we?"

The children agreed that going home would be a good idea, so they each handed their books to Emma, who placed them into her backpack and strapped it tight to her back.

Everett turned around to utter the incantation that activated the table, which the children all grew to respect during their many travels.

"*Quod est superius est sicut quod inferius!*" he shouted.

The children gathered around the table, which began to make its familiar humming sound. They were all ready to see what the real world felt like after having been away from it for so long.

Something puzzled Shiloh, though. He didn't know what those words meant or how the magic worked. He looked up to his grandfather again, whose eyes glowed in the light emanated by the runes.

"Grandpa, what does that mean?" asked Shiloh.

Everett looked at his grandson, proud to see that Shiloh was just as inquisitive as he was when he was younger.

"As above, so below."

These words held so much power in them they felt magical even to say.

"Now, let's get out of here," said Everett.

Yet Shiloh still had something on his mind.

"How are we supposed to get back home if we don't have a 'home' book?"

This brought a childish grin to Everett's wrinkled face. He told the children to stand around the table and close their eyes.

"You don't need books, Shiloh. They just help answer questions," said Everett.

"What questions?" asked Emma, confused.

"All you need," said Everett, "is to simply ask yourself when, where, and why. The table will do the rest."

None of them had expected this answer. The children quickly realized that the table held more power than they had initially thought.

"Imagine anywhere," said Everett.

A few seconds of silent thinking went by, filled with the rustling of clothes and the slowing of breath. For a moment, Emma flashed back in her mind to when she was locked in a cell, back in *Starsurfers*. This moment's stillness felt similarly nerve-racking, but she found solace in being reunited with her friends for whatever was to come.

They all squeezed their eyes shut and placed their hands on the table, which hummed louder each second, and imagined themselves going home.

Shiloh thought about his grandma, then his cat, which probably needed to be fed since he'd been gone for so long. Emma thought of her mom and how much she missed her and the things she would tell her. Logan thought, at first, of food and his kitchen. However, he quickly remembered his journey, the significance of the table, and how proud he was of his father for creating such a work of art. Logan felt regret about the way he had treated his father in the past. The boy had always been uninterested in his father, yet now there was nothing he wanted to do more than talk to him for hours on end about carpentry. Everett thought of nothing but his wife, Faith, and how badly he wanted to fix things.

As they stood around the table, hands placed on its surface, they found themselves plucking away the seeds of doubt that had taken root in their minds at the beginning of their journey. They knew that the answers to their problems would be handled in the future, not the past, and that their actions in the future would, in turn, change how they looked back at their pasts.

The sensation of the table under their palms disappeared as they held them out to touch it, and their senses were quickly filled with messages from their body to open their eyes to their new environment.

So, they did. They found themselves exactly where they thought they would end up, although they were surprised to see that their friends were gone, along with the table.

For a moment, each of them felt like they had just woken up from a dream. The world looked the same, almost as if they hadn't ever left at all.

Chapter 11
Nothing Is an Accident

Emma was now back in her old room. Her six-disc CD player was still playing songs from *Halloween, But All Year*, an album by indie singer Foreign Forest, at a low volume. The same album on the same CD she had put on before leaving to meet her friends at Shiloh's house. Emma was amazed at how little time had passed while she was gone. She turned to notice that her window was still partially opened from how she had left it. But seeing that she no longer needed it to sneak back in, she walked over and locked it shut.

Logan initially thought of many things when his eyes were closed. He thought about his home for a second, but his mind quickly directed his thinking toward his father, the table, and finally, a sandwich. When he opened his eyes, he was inside a sandwich shop that seemed very familiar. He was surprised when he realized where he was, though not ultimately disappointed. He and his father loved to eat there most evenings, though never this late. It was currently after hours, so the shop had been locked up, and Logan was stuck inside. At first, he was nervous about getting out of the store without setting off the security alarm. Still, after looking around, he found a phone to call his father from, which eased his nerves a bit. His father sounded confused at first, asking the boy how he got there in the first place, but he changed his demeanor soon after and directed Logan to unlock the front door and run outside and around the corner, where he would be waiting for him. Logan hung up the phone and quickly made himself a sandwich, using the shop's ingredients: two pieces of white bread, a stack of roast beef slices, some sprouts, tomato, and some avocado spread. The boy then unlocked the front door and ran down the street and around the corner to where his father had told him to meet.

Five minutes later, Logan's father pulled up next to him. He rolled the window down and yelled at Logan, "Get in now!"

Logan felt more nervous now after hearing his father's stern tone. He brushed off any crumbs from his face and shirt and got in the car. On his way home, two police vehicles sped past them with their sirens on, and both Logan and his father knew exactly where they were going. After two or three minutes of driving, Logan's father broke the silence.

"Why were you not home in your bed, and how the hell did you end up in Barney's?" asked Logan's father in an irritated tone.

Before receiving the phone call from his son, Logan's father was in bed. After falling asleep watching a TV show with his family, he and Logan's mother retired to their bedroom, turning the lights off and leaving their son sleeping on the couch.

"Dad, do you remember when you made that table for that weird old guy?" asked Logan.

His father looked over at him, mouth wide open. "How did you… where…" said Logan's father, now less irritated and, for the most part, confused.

As the car stopped in their driveway, Logan looked over at his father with eyes holding back tears.

"Dad, I am so sorry for how I've treated you. I've always told you I don't want to be like you when I grow up, but the whole time, I just didn't see how awesome you are. I love you, dad, and I'm sorry I just asked you to pick me up as you did. I didn't know who else to call… but I promise I will tell you everything… I know… tomorrow."

Logan yawned. He was so exhausted, and his father could see it. He wanted his son to tell him more, to make sense of the absurdity he was witnessing. Still, he appreciated his son's confession.

"I'll always have your back, buddy."

His father took Logan into his room and laid him in bed. Logan's bed was never made, so his father bent down, picked up the bedsheet on the floor, and threw it over him. As his father exited and closed the door, Logan slightly lifted an eyelid to make sure the coast was clear. He couldn't stop thinking about the journey he had embarked on, and how it was with people he knew very little of at first, who now undoubtedly hold their claim of property in his heart. He especially couldn't stop seeing Shiloh in his thoughts. He had watched his friend develop, and in turn, how he viewed him differently. He smirked as he dozed off to sleep.

Everett, who woke up in his bed, got there by thinking only of his beloved wife, Faith. He turned over to see her asleep, smiled, and shed a tear. The magician had missed his wife so much, and now that she was right here, there was so much that he wanted to tell her. Instead, he lightly kissed her forehead and fell asleep beside her, leaving their reunion for the next day.

While he was supposed to be thinking of home, Shiloh looked over at Emma, who had her eyes shut tight like the others, when suddenly, she disappeared. Only a second after, Logan and Shiloh's grandfather did the same, so Shiloh quickly closed his eyes tight and thought as hard as he could about going home, but it was no use. His mind couldn't stop thinking about Emma, whom he had grown so close to throughout their journey. He couldn't help but constantly wonder what would happen to them when they got back to the real world.

Shiloh opened his eyes, and there was Emma—or rather, the back of her head, anyway. The girl was just about to close the window to her bedroom. Emma turned and gasped at the sight of him.

"Shiloh?!" she whispered, confused and trying not to wake up her parents.

"I'm— I don't know how I— I'm so sorry," whispered Shiloh, whose face flushed with embarrassment.

Upon seeing Shiloh, Emma was confused, yet she quickly grew accustomed to his company.

"It's okay. I don't mind. I think my mom is asleep, anyway," said Emma.

Shiloh let out a sigh of relief and sat down on the edge of Emma's bed.

"How long do you think we were gone?" she asked as she stared out of the window, brushing her hair behind her ear and then turning to look at him.

"I'm not sure. It's still late out, like when we left."

Trillions of stars lit the sky and illuminated Emma's room, giving life to the vibrant navy-blue paint that seemed black in the shadows.

"How, though? I thought we've been gone for days," said Emma as she walked across the room to her bed.

She sat down for a moment with a puzzled look on her face, then soon after, grabbed her laptop from under her pillow. She opened it up, then connected the device to her family's Wi-Fi, which allowed her time and date settings to update.

"It's three in the morning," said Emma, confused.

According to her laptop, she and her friend's time away from home had only cost them about four hours in the real world.

"That's either the scariest or the coolest thing ever, if you think about it. My grandpa has been missing for over a year… Do you think he's lived more than most people?" asked Shiloh, perplexed.

"Probably," said Emma. "But WOW! He must've felt so lonely."

Shiloh sighed and nodded. He walked over to where Emma was sitting on the bed and sat next to her.

The boy was feeling nervous, as one usually would be around someone they'd had a crush on for quite some time. The past few days (or hours) away from home kept playing in his head, and one moment that stood out was when they were in the white world of nothing, the in-between reality created by the table just for them. Emma assured Shiloh that she wasn't going anywhere and that she would stick by his side through and through.

As the boy sat beside Emma in her room, they both exchanged glances while busying their hands. Shiloh was playing with Emma's shoelaces while Emma was twirling her hair. Things had changed for them both, and Shiloh realized now that reality was simply what one made of it.

That thought gave him the courage to place his hand on hers.

She cleared her throat.

"You know, Shiloh," said Emma in a lighter, more playful tone, "you're tougher than you look."

Shiloh couldn't tell if that was meant as a compliment or an insult, but he smiled anyway.

"You're like…"

A few seconds passed as Shiloh tried to find the right words. Emma smiled as she noticed him staring intensely at the ceiling, the floor, and then finally at her. Something connected them in that moment, whether it be the moonlight that flooded the room, the magic of the table, or even young love in bloom.

Shiloh, unable to conjure up the magic necessary to strike a kiss, remembered that he needed only to ask himself the questions: when, where, and why. Shiloh leaned in and kissed Emma, who leaned in, as well, and grabbed his face as she kissed him back.

Both of them collapsed onto the bed and continued kissing, Emma adjusting her position to be on top of Shiloh. Thirty minutes had passed, and after noticing that Emma's CD player had stopped, Shiloh sat up and broke the lock of their lips, his face a mix of pride and confusion.

"I'm sorry," whispered Shiloh, unsure if he was being too forward or not.

"I'm not," said Emma, who grabbed Shiloh's face once more, kissing him twice as hard as before.

He relinquished his say over the matter and gave in.

It was quiet in Emma's house, and their whispers didn't travel very far, but there was a faint thumping sound coming from the floorboards every few seconds, which made Emma break the kiss.

"But…" said Emma with a smile, "I think my mom might've woken up, so let's pick this up tomorrow, yeah?"

Shiloh quickly gathered himself to leave before Emma's mother discovered him and made his way out of the window, receiving a kiss on the cheek as he stuck his feet out to feel for the ground beneath him outside. Emma's kiss made him hit his head on the window frame, causing them both to laugh as he finessed his way out.

Shiloh began his walk back home on a dimly lit gravel road, turning around one last time to look at Emma's window, which was now just a tiny blur. After the past couple of hours, he was now about ninety-nine percent sure that what had just happened was real, and that was enough for him. The mountains of doubt in Shiloh's mind had cleared out, making room for the new "mountains" he'd climb in the coming days. His walk home soon turned into a run, and the fresh air on his face brought him back to life as he pushed through the first rays of dawn.

Shiloh had made it home in about fifteen minutes, which was odd because, by car, he knew it would've taken about twenty. He was excited to see what the future would bring for him and his friends, and as he threw his shirt onto his bedroom floor before lying in bed, he started humming a song. He was wiggling his toes back and forth with pleasure, laying with his hands behind his head, playing reruns in his mind of when he kissed Emma, and she kissed him back.

Lucious, Shiloh's cat, hopped on the bed and rested on his chest, demanding the affection he was deprived of for the past few hours.

Though he was in bed, Shiloh had no idea how he would get any rest with the thought of tomorrow on his mind, but with the motion of time in full swing here in the real world, it didn't take long for him to fall asleep. He thought about his parents as he drifted off, whom he had missed deeply, and whose faces were clearer now more than ever. The thought of Emma returned, though, and his mind oscillated between seeing his parents and spending time with her.

While considering how unreal and limitless the past few days in the books had felt, Shiloh settled on the notion that the "real" world, too, could become whatever he wanted it to be. This little secret made him grin before he fell asleep, knowing that he could see, hear, smell, touch, and taste anything he could think of, and it wouldn't make a difference whether or not his eyes were open.

137

QUOD EST SUPERIUS EST SICUT QUOD INFERIUS.